STARTING ANEW

LOVE UNEXPECTED
BOOK 3

MELANIE D. SNITKER

DALLIONZ MEDIA, LLC

Starting Anew
(Love Unexpected: Book 3)
© 2019 Melanie D. Snitker

Published by
Dallionz Media, LLC
P.O. Box 5283
Abilene, TX 79608

Cover: Blue Valley Author Services

For permission requests, please contact the author at the e-mail below or through her website.

Melanie D. Snitker
melanie@melaniedsnitker.com
www.melaniedsnitker.com

This is a work of fiction. Names, characters, businesses, places, events, and incidents either are the products of the author's imagination or used in a fictitious manner. Any resemblance to actual persons, living or dead, or actual events is purely coincidental.

Therefore, if anyone is in Christ,
he is a new creation;
old things have passed away;
behold, all things have become new.
2 Corinthians 5:17 (NKJ)

1

L ynn Crosby sat up in bed, unsure of what actually woke her up. Her heart pounded as she held her breath. A scratching sound floated to her from somewhere inside the small house she rented. Immediately, the blood rushing in her ears competed with her ability to tell which direction the scratching came from.

No, not again.

She pictured someone using a crowbar to pry open the door. Or maybe a window. Sure, they were locked: Lynn made sure of that before she went to bed every night. But would that stop someone with the right tool and enough determination? She knew from experience that it wouldn't.

More scratching noises. She should've known her past would catch up to her eventually.

Well, she couldn't very well just sit, frozen, in her bed while she waited for the inevitable.

She'd slept with a baseball bat by her bed for more than two years. Then she started to relax again, and consciously put it away as a sign of moving on, and now she couldn't remember where. Not the smartest move she'd ever made. If she couldn't find the bat in the morning, she'd buy a new one. Lynn gathered her strength, and her cell phone, and crept out of her bedroom. She paused in the hallway again. Moments later, more scratching told her it was coming from the back door.

Once in the kitchen, she flipped the light on. With any luck, an intruder would see that and run for the hills. The scratching continued.

Fabulous. If turning the light on didn't scare the intruder away, then not much was going to deter him.

Lynn's mouth went dry as her gaze landed on the large marble rolling pin her friend Sharon had given her as a joke last Christmas. Lynn didn't bake. At all. But she'd kept the fancy rolling pin on the kitchen counter because it looked nice.

She lifted it, thankful for the weight in her hand. Yes, this was sure to knock someone out.

"Okay, God," she whispered as she made her way to the back door. "Help me out here. I really don't want to die in my pajamas."

She put a hand on the door knob before speaking loudly. "I've got a weapon, and I will use it. Step away from the door."

Silence. These were the times when Lynn wished she were married. Having a strong, protective man in the house would be great right about now. Then maybe he'd be wielding something a little more effective than a rolling pin as he stood between her and the intruder at the door…

Lynn pulled one slat of the mini blinds up and glanced outside as she turned the porch light on. Nothing. The scratching had ceased. Maybe the sheer ferocity in her voice had scared the intruder away.

She'd just released a lungful of air and turned away when

a long scratch against the door made her jump a foot. She nearly dropped the rolling pin, an act that surely would've broken her foot or cracked the tile below.

"Meeeeeoooooowwww."

The soulful wail of a cat simultaneously flooded Lynn's system with relief and annoyance. "You've got to be kidding me."

With the rolling pin still in one hand, she opened the back door to find a Siamese kitten staring up at her with bright blue eyes. "Meow."

And then, as if the cat had lived in Lynn's house all its life, it walked right through the door and into the kitchen with a swish of its tail.

"Well come right in, your highness." Lynn made sure to lock the back door again before turning to find the kitten sitting on her kitchen counter. "You know, I just about used this thing for the first time tonight." She shook the rolling pin for emphasis before placing it in the wooden cradle where it belonged. Lynn glanced at the clock on the microwave. Two-thirty on Friday morning. She sighed. "Visiting hours don't start until seven."

As soon as Lynn came within an arm's length of the cat, its little purr-box started up. Lynn had always been a sucker for a purring cat. She ran a hand over the soft fur as her heart melted. She picked up the kitten and turned it over on its back to see whether it was a boy or a girl.

"I really should toss you back outside, mister." Lynn stifled a yawn. "But I don't need you scratching at my back door again."

She set him on the floor and turned lights off on the way back to her bedroom. The cat bounded past her and onto the bed where he sat expectantly. "Fine, just for tonight. Please don't have fleas. Or pee on my bed."

Lynn set her alarm for an hour earlier than usual before climbing beneath the covers. The kitten curled up next to her. The last thing Lynn registered before she fell asleep again was how having that warm little body lying next to her made her feel more relaxed than she had in a long time.

———

LYNN TRIED to blink the sleep from her eyes later that morning as she popped the last bite of muffin into her mouth and grabbed her bag. The kitten meowed at her, as though asking to come along.

"Nope, you get to hold down the fort. I'll be back later." Lynn reached down and scratched the cat behind his ears.

On her way through the living room to the front door, she paused and let a hand rest on the electronic keyboard tucked against one wall. A thin layer of dust covered the surface triggering a twinge of regret. There was a time when she wouldn't have dreamed of neglecting it like this. It'd been way too long since she'd run a cloth over the instrument, and even longer since she'd played it.

A part of her needed to sit and let her fingers dance over the keys as the world melted away. At least, that's the way her music used to affect her. Now, just thinking about it made dread pool in the pit of her stomach. Both sides of her warred so strongly against each other, that it was easier for Lynn to push the whole idea from her mind.

She'd at least dust it tonight when she got home. Pretending that made her feel better, Lynn turned her back on what used to be an extension of herself, left the house, and locked the door behind her.

Not long later, she pulled into the parking lot of the Little Lambs Christian Daycare and Preschool where she'd been working for the last two years. She liked this part of Fort Worth because it felt more like a small town rather than part of one of the largest metropolitan areas in Texas.

Before getting out of her pale blue Volkswagen Beetle, she automatically did a quick scan of the parking lot and street. It took several moments before she realized what she'd done. Lynn released a heavy sigh. She'd finally stopped scoping out parking lots six months ago. The cat scaring her had also reawakened her anxiety. And here Lynn thought she'd moved past it.

"Apparently not."

Annoyed and muttering to herself, she finished a visual perusal of the parking lot. Convinced all was well, she got out and walked to the building.

It'd been over two years since she'd left her old life as an artist in the music business. Singing as lead in a pop group had her in frequent spotlights, and her parents hated it. They hated everything about the career path Lynn had chosen.

Music was everything, but there'd been a variety of reasons why she'd left it all in the past. When their lead guitarist was busted for drug possession, the rest of the group fell apart, and it only confirmed her decision.

Unfortunately, it also solidified the opinion of Lynn's parents when it came to her career. By the time things settled down, they still wanted nothing to do with her, and certainly didn't want Lynn's influence on her little sister's life.

It'd been over two years since she'd assumed a new name. Two years of life out of the spotlight and away from reporters trying to dig up more dirt on her. She missed music —missed her family—but a slower lifestyle was a huge relief.

Thankfully, her boss and friend, Sharon, had understood Lynn's situation when she hired her. Background checks were run on Lynn's real name, Bethany Truitt, but she went by

Lynn Crosby otherwise. The only other person who knew was her landlord.

It always took Lynn a moment to adjust when going from the too-quiet house she rented to the bustling activity of Little Lambs. The large building attached to Fort Worth Christian Church was home to multiple classrooms as well as the nursery where Lynn worked. While she enjoyed interacting with children of any age, she'd always been drawn to the little ones.

She'd chosen childcare for a variety of reasons, but ultimately found spending her day cuddling babies and making them smile was just plain fun. Besides, it was about as different from her previous career as she could get. Not only that, but parents were tired and hurried when they dropped their children off, making it less likely any of them would recognize Lynn from her time in the spotlight. It was the perfect job.

Sharon saw Lynn enter and waved. Lynn returned the greeting and spotted Trina waiting to check her young son in at the front counter. Lynn stowed her belongings and headed that direction.

Trina held eight-week-old Brian in one arm while she finished signing in. When she turned to Lynn, Trina appeared hesitant as she held her baby close and kept looking down at him.

Lynn took the baby and cradled him in her arms. He slept soundly, a peaceful look on his face. Trina ran a finger over his chubby cheek.

"I hate leaving him." She frowned, regret filling her voice. "It's been two weeks since I went back to work. I thought I'd be getting used to it by now."

Lynn might've given Trina a hug if she didn't already have her arms full. Parents used Little Lambs for many different reasons. Lynn could imagine how hard it would be to leave her baby for the day. Usually it was more difficult for the parents than it was for the child. "I promise I'll call you if anything comes up. We have your cell and work numbers. We'll get a hold of you if we need to."

Trina nodded. "I know. I appreciate it." She finally looked up from her son to meet Lynn's eyes. "I'm sorry I'm always such a mess."

"You're not a mess. Brian is lucky to have a mom who loves him so much."

That seemed to make Trina feel better. She finally placed a last kiss to her son's cheek. "Love you, buddy. See you soon." After a lingering look, she turned and left the building.

Lynn yawned into her shoulder so she wouldn't disturb her tiny charge. There were several cribs set up in the nursery to provide comfortable places for the babies to sleep. She transferred Brian and waited long enough to see he continued to sleep. She knew he would awaken in the next half hour or so for a diaper change and a bottle.

She yawned again, and this time Sharon noticed. "Someone might think you were the one with an infant at home keeping you up at all hours of the night."

"Right?" Lynn used to think she'd settle down and get married one day. Except nothing about her life had gone the way she'd planned when she was young. "I was up at two-thirty in the morning protecting my house from an intruding kitten with nothing but courage and a rolling pin."

Oh, if only Sharon could see the incredulous look on her face right now. Lynn chuckled at her friend.

Sharon set a bottle onto the table next to the rocking chair she was in and situated the infant she held onto her shoulder. "Okay, you're going to have to start from the beginning." She gently patted the baby's back.

Lynn related her middle-of-the-night adventures. "Then I had to get up early to go to the store and buy a litter box and cat food before work. I just hope he's not tearing my place up right now." She groaned. At least he hadn't gone to the bathroom anywhere she could find. Hopefully this kitten came litter-box trained.

Sharon was laughing now. "And here I hoped you were tired because you were out on a hot date last night. Instead, you're on the fast track to becoming the neighborhood cat lady. You've got to get out more."

"Gee, thanks for that." One kitten did not a cat lady make. "It might be nice to have the little purr box to come home to." Lynn was perfectly content with her life. Sure, she left work at the day care center and spent most evenings alone. She had her exercise routine, her favorite TV shows streaming, and a stack of books on her nightstand to read. Okay, maybe she was forcing herself to feel content. But wasn't that better than being miserable?

Sharon gave Lynn a knowing look. "I'm serious, Lynn. People aren't meant to be alone. I get why you were lying low for a while. But everything has blown over. No offense, but I doubt anyone would recognize you now. You need to start living your life again instead of letting the past dictate it for you."

Ouch.

Lynn gave her friend a good-natured glare. She wanted to argue with Sharon, but she had little ammunition. Sharon was right.

What had been necessary had transformed into a comfortable habit for Lynn. That wasn't a good thing. Over the years, the mess surrounding her group had faded into the background, their album fell off the charts, and interest in Lynn had fizzled to nothing. After everything that happened, it's what she wanted. To go back to being just another normal person.

It seemed the only people who hadn't forgotten were her parents.

Sharon's expression softened. "You know I'm just worried about you. What you need is to take a class or two somewhere. You should seriously consider some form of martial arts. Then next time, you don't have to resort to using the rolling pin." She chuckled to herself. "Of course, since it's not being used for anything else…"

"Funny. Real funny." Lynn made a face at her friend. "You know those posts that go around where you say the one thing that would help friends and family know you've been replaced by aliens?" She paused for effect. "For me, that would be cooking. If I post or say I'm trying a new recipe or baking something, you know the real me has been abducted."

That had Sharon laughing hard. "Isn't that the truth?" She fanned herself as she continued to rock the infant in her arms. "You know, Walt has a younger brother. Maybe we could all go out for dinner one night."

Lynn shot her an exasperated look. "I'm not interested, Sharon. No matter who it is."

"Most guys would understand where you're coming from if you just told them what was going on."

Lynn wasn't so sure that was true, and it wasn't as easy as Sharon made it out to be. If Lynn introduced herself by her given name, she'd risk that person knowing who she was and making assumptions based on the past. It'd be easier to get to know the guy first, except she'd have to explain the whole situation later.

She sighed with the complexity of it all.

A deep voice carried from the front of the building and

sent Lynn's heart into a full gallop. She glanced at Sharon and found her friend grinning, a knowing look on her face.

"You should ask him out," Sharon whispered as Lynn walked by.

It was a good thing Lynn loved her friend so much. She squared her shoulders as she made her way to the front. There's no way she could ask Nathan Kirkpatrick on a date. He was a single dad, and Lynn took care of his daughter while he worked. That was complicated enough without throwing her mess of a past into the blender.

She rounded the corner and swallowed hard. Nathan was signing in at the front counter while balancing his daughter in the other arm. Mia cried in earnest as she clung to her daddy's shoulder. The shirt he wore had dark stains where the eleven-month-old's tears had soaked the fabric.

Nathan was one of the nicest, most attractive men she'd ever met. Not that it mattered, because Lynn wasn't about to ask him out on a date.

He put the pen on the counter, spotted Lynn, and immediately gave her an apologetic look. "I'm sorry. We had a rough morning." He wrinkled his nose. "And I promise she had a clean diaper when we left the house. I can change her before I go…"

Between the way he glanced at the clock on the wall and then at his daughter's face, it was obvious he was running late. Lynn shook her head. "It's okay. I can take care of it." She held her hands out for Mia, but the girl continued to wail in her dad's arms. "I'll be right back."

There was a particular stuffed dog that Mia carried around with her nearly every day. Lynn found it and brought it to the front. "Mia, are you ready to come play with Woof-Woof? He's been waiting to see you all morning."

Mia hiccupped as she lifted her head and looked at the

stuffed dog, her bright blue eyes still swimming with tears. They were the exact same color as her dad's, not that Lynn had noticed. Much.

Between her eyes, that tousled blonde hair, and those slightly-pointed ears, she looked like a little pixie. Lynn's heart melted just like it did every time she saw the girl.

Mia finally released her hold on Nathan's arm and reached for Lynn. When Lynn took the baby, her hands brushed against Nathan's, sending tingles dancing along her arms. For just a moment, she caught a whiff of his woodsy scent. She always wondered if it was his deodorant or the aftershave he used.

She got to enjoy it for a moment before Mia's dirty diaper enveloped Lynn in an entirely different aroma. Lynn did her best to maintain a straight face and not wrinkle her nose.

Nathan grabbed the diaper bag at his feet and handed it over. "Again, I'm sorry to drop her off like this. The morning got away from us."

"It really is okay. We've got this, don't we, Mia?" She looked at the little girl who hugged Woof-Woof tightly in her arms. "Can you wave bye to Daddy?"

Mia sniffed and waved with one hand.

"Goodbye, baby. I'll see you this evening. Be good for Miss Lynn."

With one last look, he ran his hand through his short-cropped, dark blond hair, turned, and left.

Lynn was still trying to ignore the way her insides turned to jelly every time Nathan said her name when Mia started to cry again. Tears rolled down her cheeks as she stared at the door.

"Oh, Mia. It's alright. Come on, let's go get you cleaned up." Lynn carried her into the nursery to find Sharon watching her with amusement. "Don't even start."

Sharon waited long enough to be certain no one would overhear her. "You should think about it. I'll bet he's not a whole lot older than you. Mia adores you, which is a huge plus in your favor."

Lynn rubbed Mia's back as she made her way to the changing table. "And getting involved with the parent of one of our kids wouldn't be messy at all." She turned her back on her friend to tend to Mia, ending the conversation.

She secured a new diaper, slipped Mia's pants back on, and stood her up on her feet. "There we go. I'll bet that feels so much better. Come on, bug, let's go find something for you to play with."

So what if Lynn had a crush on Nathan? She'd seen him five days a week for the last five months, and he'd never shown an ounce of interest in her. It was best if Lynn continued to take care of Mia and admire Nathan from afar.

———

JEB FRANKLIN TOOK a long swig from a bottle of beer and set it back down on his desk with a thud. Not once did he take his eyes off the computer monitor.

He allowed the music to wash over him, but it wasn't just that. Bethany Truitt sang like an angel. Her fingers flew across the electronic keyboard as words he knew well flowed from her mouth.

He'd memorized every second of the video, from the moments she took in a deep breath to the bridge where she let her hands drop to her side as her eyelids fell slightly and she sang from her heart.

Bethany always sang from her heart.

Jeb wasn't sure which he loved more: The sound of her

voice, or the way she'd occasionally look right at the camera, as though her hazel eyes were fixed on him alone.

When the song was over, he switched tabs in his browser and began his nightly scour of social media. Ever since Bethany went off the radar years ago, he'd been watching hashtags hoping to catch a hint of where she might be now. False alarms in the past had led him as far as Florida and Idaho in search of the love of his life.

If only she'd start singing and touring again. He'd follow her from town to town like he used to. But this time, he wouldn't come on as strong. Every time he thought about trying to break into her bus, he wanted to kick himself.

Bethany was high class. She deserved to be courted as such. No more heavy-handed attempts to get her to notice him. He had to win her over.

He opened his desk drawer, revealing a large collection of guitar pics with Bethany's name on them. He'd collected one or two from every concert he'd attended. One of these days, he'd find her again. Then he'd show her just how devoted he was. Eventually, she'd take notice of him. She'd realize that she loved him just as much as he did her.

Then they could finally be happy together.

Jeb finished his now-warm beer, closed the desk drawer again, and re-opened the previous browser. With a smile, he selected another video.

2

———

Nathan slid into the cab of his Jeep Wrangler and rolled a window down. Leave it to Texas to jump the gun on spring. It was the first week of March, and temperature highs were expected to be in the eighties. He'd have to make a point of taking Mia outside to play on Sunday before it got too hot.

Guilt tugged at him as he drove away from Little Lambs. He hated leaving Mia upset like that. These were the mornings when he wished he could keep Mia with him, or that she had a mother at home to care for her.

Being a single dad was anything but easy. He was doing his best to raise Mia with the love and support he lacked throughout his own childhood. Thankfully, Mia had Nathan's brother and his family to be there for her, too.

And to hand his daughter over with a dirty diaper... Nathan groaned. It was Lynn's job to look after Mia, change her diaper, and care for her during the day. But she shouldn't have to start off like that. He had to hand it to her for keeping a smile on her face. She seemed to manage anything that came at her with a measure of grace.

He thought about the way her smile deepened that cute dimple in her chin. He wasn't sure which he liked better: her dimple, the pretty dark hair that framed her face, or the way her expressive hazel eyes made him wish he knew her better.

He realized he was grinning and sobered with a sigh.

It didn't matter how beautiful Lynn was, he wasn't in the market for a relationship. If there was one thing Mia's mother, Gwen, taught him, it's that you can never really know a person. Especially when you start throwing love in the mix. Back then, he'd thought he loved Gwen. She'd proved him wrong when she willingly walked away from him and their daughter without looking back. Nathan had been angry with her—furious even—but he'd never suffered from a broken heart. Clearly he hadn't been as in love with her as he'd thought.

It was bad enough Mia's mother hadn't wanted her. What made it worse was that something similar happened to him as well. If there was one thing he'd promised Mia, it was that he'd stay by her no matter what. The cycle would stop now, and Mia would grow up with a parent devoted to raising her and loving her the way she deserved.

First his own adoptive parents, and then Gwen, had been dishonest with Nathan. That was one of his pet peeves, and he promised he'd raise Mia in honesty. She wouldn't grow up wondering whether her daddy was telling her the truth or not.

The last thing he needed was to put Mia in a position where she could get more attached to Lynn than she already was, only to have Lynn eventually walk away. At least now she saw Lynn in a more professional situation, even if Mia really was too young to know the difference.

If—and that was a big if—Nathan decided to start dating, Lynn would be off limits.

Nathan drove the ten miles through Fort Worth morning

traffic to the Brazilian Jiu-Jitsu Academy where he worked as an instructor. He'd only recently moved to the area in October and was able to secure this job thanks to the recommendation of his instructor back in Miami. It'd been a big change making this kind of a move, but it'd been worth it to be near his brother and future sister-in-law.

His phone rang, and Chess's name popped up. Nathan chuckled at the timing. "Hey, Chess. What's going on?" He looked at the clock. The first class of the day started in half an hour. He moved to put his things away in one of the lockers.

"Did you double check with Gregor about having the wedding off?"

Nathan's boss was notorious for forgetting to write things down. "I did, and we're all set. Two weeks from tomorrow—you're not getting cold feet, I hope."

Chess chuckled. "Not on your life. You ask Lynn to watch Mia yet?"

Nathan closed the locker door a little too loudly. "Not yet." Since Nathan was in the wedding party along with the rest of Chess's family, that meant Nathan needed to find someone to sit with Mia at the ceremony. Lynn's name had come up at one point. Honestly, Nathan was hoping another option would present itself. It was one thing to ignore his attraction to Lynn when she was working for Little Lambs. It'd be an entirely different situation if she were there with the rest of Nathan's family.

"You know, if you asked her out on a date or two before the wedding, it might not be so awkward. Or better yet, bring her to dinner tomorrow night."

Nathan cringed. According to his brother, Nathan talked a little too frequently about Lynn. Once Chess mentioned it to his fiancé, Brooke, Nathan hadn't heard the end of it.

Chess's voice came through the phone. "Seriously, Anna said she could hold Mia if you want her to."

Anna was going to be Brooke's maid of honor. It'd be no easier for her to hold Mia than it would be for Nathan, who was standing as Chess's best man.

There really was no one else to ask. If Nathan had to leave Mia with someone in the audience, it needed to be someone she knew, and Nathan really couldn't think of anyone more perfect for the job than Lynn. But if he didn't ask her soon, he'd be too late and out of options.

"Nah, I'll ask Lynn to watch her when I pick Mia up."

"Good. I'll let you go and see you tomorrow."

"Yep. Bye, Chess."

The decision made, Nathan turned his focus on the students gathering on the mats. Among the many classes the academy offered for kids, Nathan taught one specifically for the local homeschool group. It'd become so popular, they decided to set up a second one for beginners and move those who were more advanced into a class of their own.

Nathan looked at the new faces sitting in front of him and smiled. "Welcome, everyone. I'm happy to see you all here today. People learn a form of martial arts for a lot of different reasons. Why don't we go around and each of you tell me your name and why you want to learn Brazilian jiu-jitsu."

He pointed at the boy nearest him who shared his information. Nathan made a mental note of each child's name as they spoke, certain he'd have to go through the roster at least another time or two before he'd have them all memorized. When all but one boy had answered, Nathan motioned to him. "How about you?"

The boy, who looked to be eleven or twelve, crossed his arms in front of him. "I'm Lee, and I'm here because my mom is making me."

Nathan glanced to the side where a bunch of parents were sitting. There was no mistaking Lee's mother when she gave Nathan a look of apology.

"You know what? That's okay." He walked back and forth in front of the kids before stopping again in front of Lee. "When I first started to learn jiu-jitsu, it was about the last thing I felt like doing. I was in a lot of trouble in school, and I hated the world." Nathan could see a lot of himself in Lee from his body posture to the hardness in the boy's eyes. "But I had an instructor who didn't let me slack off and who taught me how to gain confidence in myself. He never gave up on me, and I have no intention of giving up on any of you, either." Nathan pointed a finger at the whole class.

Lee looked doubtful, but Nathan took that as a challenge as he began to explain the history of jiu-jitsu and what he planned to teach them over the next few months.

By the end of the day, Nathan had taught five more classes and was more than ready to pick up Mia and ask Lynn if she'd keep his daughter during the wedding.

THANKFULLY, when Nathan arrived to pick up Mia, she looked a lot happier than when he'd left. He found her standing next to a play stove. The moment she saw him, she gave him a wave with her chubby arm followed by, "Da! Da!" No matter how rough his day might be, hearing that word and seeing her sweet smile made it all worthwhile.

He sat on the floor beside her. She toddled his way and fell into his arms. Nathan blew a raspberry on her cheek that had her belly laughing.

A shadow fell over them before Lynn knelt on the floor beside them. "She did great today. She was tired and took an early nap. Once she woke up from that, it was full steam ahead." She smiled, the dimple in her chin drawing Nathan's attention. "We had fun, didn't we, bug?" She reached over and patted Mia's back before standing again. "Let me get her bag for you."

Nathan was determined to ask her this time and cleared his throat. "I actually have a question for you."

"Okay." She eased herself onto the floor again and sat cross legged, her eyes on him.

He couldn't quite tell if they were more brown or green, or an exact mix of the two. He wanted to stare into them way longer than was appropriate. "My brother's getting married two weeks from Saturday. I'm in the wedding party along with the rest of Mia's family. It would be a huge help to have someone in the audience to watch over Mia during the ceremony." He swallowed. "I wondered if it were possible to hire you to come watch her for a few hours. You'd be in the same building I'm in, and of course I'd pay you."

"Oh. Well…" Lynn looked at Mia.

He was rambling and wasn't sure if the look on her face was surprise or confusion. "I know it's short notice. If you have other plans, I'd understand. I just wanted to ask you first since Mia knows you so well. I thought it'd be easier on her to not have to get used to a stranger." Nathan held his breath. It was ridiculous how much he hoped she'd say yes.

She nodded then but kept her gaze on everything but him. "I have that day free. I'd be happy to help. Is it in the area?"

"It's in Dallas. I'll pay you for six hours. That should more than cover the drive each way plus the time during the ceremony."

Lynn finally lifted her eyes and locked gazes with him. "That sounds great."

They talked and settled on a figure, which truthfully was lower than he'd expected.

"There will be a reception afterward. You're welcome to attend. It'll be an informal barbecue. If you have someone you'd like to bring, you're welcome to a plus one." He'd noted months ago that she didn't wear a wedding ring. That didn't mean there wasn't a significant other hiding in the shadows, though.

"I won't have a plus one." She got to her feet and brushed some of her hair behind one ear. "Let me go grab Mia's things for you."

He stood and lifted Mia into his arms. Lynn returned momentarily, and he accepted the diaper bag from her. "Thanks, I appreciate it."

He was going to tell her he'd bring all the information for her on Monday but paused. Chess's words went through his head, and before Nathan knew it, words were flowing out of his mouth. "I work on Saturdays, and my brother and his fiancée watch Mia. After I get off work, we all meet there for dinner. If you'd like to come, we'd be happy to have you."

When she looked surprised, he rushed on. "It'd give you a chance to meet everyone before the wedding. It might also be helpful for Mia to see you outside of daycare. That way she won't be surprised when she sees you at the church."

He hadn't expected the complete turmoil of emotions that danced across her eyes. What had he been thinking? If she agreed, was he supposed to just give her the address? Offer to drive her himself?

Lynn seemed to sort through her options before shifting her weight and looking at the clock. "I suppose that would be helpful. I don't drive in Dallas all that often, so getting a feel for the area where the church is, especially, would be a good thing. Do you think you could give me the addresses for both?"

"Of course." His relief when she said she'd join him was immediate and more intense than he'd expected. He told himself that it was entirely because he knew Mia would be more comfortable if she spent extra time with Lynn. "I'll call Chess or Brooke and get the church address. Then I can text that to you along with my brother's. If you'd prefer, I'd be happy to swing by and pick you up on the way there."

She ran the fingers of her right hand through that dark hair of hers before answering. "Sending me the addresses will be great, thank you."

Was it because she preferred to drive herself, or because she'd rather he not know where she lived? The question was way more interesting than it ought to be.

They verified the time and exchanged numbers before Nathan pocketed his phone. "I'll see you tomorrow evening."

"Yeah. See you then." She waved at Mia, her freckled nose wrinkled as she made a funny face that had the baby giggling.

Nathan fought against the wave of affection he experienced as he watched them interact. He picked up the diaper bag and carried his daughter out to the Jeep where he got her buckled in.

As he slid into the driver's seat, all he could think about was Lynn. She was single. Considering how sweet and beautiful she was, plus her skills with kids, how was that even possible?

He headed for home and tried to ignore the way his pulse sped up at the thought of seeing Lynn tomorrow.

3

Lynn kicked herself all day Saturday morning for agreeing to watch Mia during the wedding. Well, for that, but even more so for accepting Nathan's invitation to join them for dinner tonight. Seriously, who crashes a family dinner like that? She could hardly act normal around Nathan during the short periods she saw him at Little Lambs, what made her think she could keep her cool in a more laid-back setting? The last thing she needed was for Nathan to realize she had some silly schoolgirl crush on him.

Lynn groaned and flopped onto the couch she'd been pacing around for the last half hour. So she'd agreed in a moment of weakness. She could still back out, right? She'd text Nathan and tell him she got home and realized she already had something going on that Saturday of the wedding. Laundry and a good book counted, right?

No, he'd already mentioned that he knew it was last minute asking her as it was. She couldn't back out now, not without putting him in a bind. She sighed. "I'm pathetic."

As if in answer, the kitten jumped lightly onto the couch and curled up on Lynn's chest with a meow.

Lynn ran her hand along his back as he nuzzled her chin with his nose. "Seriously, has my life boiled down to lying here in my house talking to a cat without a name?" Only the sound of his purrs responded. He stared at her with his blue eyes as though he understood every single word she said.

Sharon was right. Lynn needed to get a life. She should probably name the cat, too, while she was at it. "How about Ninja?" The kitten sneezed, and it looked like he shook his head. Lynn chuckled. "Okay, not Ninja. Hmmm…" A regular name like Smoky or Stormy didn't seem to fit.

She went to her laptop, brought up her favorite search engine, and typed in, "Popular names for Siamese cats."

One of the first results said it included the top two hundred names. Surely she could narrow it down from there. But when she scanned through the first list of names for male Siamese cats, her gaze immediately zeroed in on the name Nathan.

And why shouldn't the name of the guy she was thinking about way too often appear on a Siamese cat website?

Lynn glanced at the kitten as he strolled into the room. "I'm not naming you Nathan."

She scrolled through the list of suggested names and stopped. "What about Thai?"

The kitten just sat and watched her as though he were waiting for her to do something more interesting.

The more Lynn thought about it, the more she liked it. "Thai. I think it fits." She turned back to the computer and shifted in the chair. "Good, now that we have that figured out, I guess we'd better make some lunch."

That decision made, she warmed up leftovers from the night before and settled down to watch some of her favorite shows on television to help pass the time.

That evening, as she followed the GPS directions to

Nathan's brother's house, Lynn again wished there were some way she could get out of this whole arrangement. Unless little Mia screamed bloody murder at seeing Lynn tonight, there was little Lynn could do.

She rubbed one sweaty palm against her jeans before gripping the steering wheel with it and wiping the other palm.

On second thought, it was one dinner. How bad could it be? Okay, it was one dinner with the guy she'd secretly liked for months. But she'd kept those feelings to herself this long, what was one more night? Or even one more week or month? No one else had to know.

Her stomach clenched in response. No matter how convinced her mind was of that fact, her heart wasn't so sure. She'd be lucky if she could eat a bite the way she felt right now.

Lynn followed the prompts from her phone as she entered a neighborhood and finally parked at the curb in front a one-story brick house. She double checked the address before grabbing the tray of brownies in the passenger seat. She stepped out of her car and walking up the paved path from the sidewalk to the red front door.

Please, God, at least let me have the right house.

She'd just raised a hand to knock when the door opened. Lynn looked up into Nathan's piercing blue eyes and swallowed hard.

"Hey, you find the place okay?"

"I did." Lynn waited until Nathan stood back. She went inside and paused while her eyes adjusted to the change in light.

"Everyone's out back. Chess is grilling steaks—his specialty—and we should be set to eat before too long." Nathan reached for her brownies. "I can take those and put them in the kitchen."

"Sure." She relinquished the baked goods. Part of her wanted to wish she'd baked something herself. But yeah, no. Store-bought brownies were as good as it got for her. When he returned, she glanced at the front door and almost wishing she could make a run for it. "I really don't want to intrude..."

"Believe it or not, I remember how weird it was walking through my brother's door back before I knew everyone last year. Trust me, if they could welcome me with open arms, you'll be fine." He winked at her. "Come on, let me introduce you."

So he hadn't known his brother before last year? Interesting.

He led the way through the house to the back door, and Lynn followed reluctantly. D*on't let any of them recognize me.*

As they stepped into the large backyard, four sets of eyes watched her along with little Mia who was being held in a woman's arms. It took the little one a few moments to realize who Lynn was before she grinned with delight and stretched her arms out.

Normally Lynn wouldn't hesitate to take the baby, but she had no idea who was holding her. She knew that Nathan was a single dad, but what if Mia's mom was still in the picture?

The woman stood from the bench of a picnic table she'd been sitting on and stretched out a hand. "Hi. You must be Lynn." When Mia continued to reach for Lynn, the woman relinquished the baby. "I'm Brooke."

Ah, Nathan's future sister-in-law. Okay, that made Lynn feel a little better. She shook Brooke's hand with a smile. "It's nice to meet you." She tickled Mia's arm and got a giggle in response. "Hey, bug. I'll bet it's weird seeing me here, isn't it?"

Other than that first confused look, Mia acted as though it

was the most natural thing in the world to have Lynn there with everyone else. She seemed content to stay in Lynn's arms, so Lynn settled the baby on her hip. "Your house is beautiful." The backyard was shaded by several large trees.

Brooke grinned. "Thank you." She nodded toward the tiny back porch. "Chess promised to build a larger deck before too long. Once he does, I'll look forward to planting a bunch of flowers." She snagged one of the guys and pulled him over. "Speaking of which, this is my fiancé, Chess."

With the exception of some subtle similarities in facial features, Chess looked nothing like his brother. He smiled, his hazel eyes sparkling. "We're happy to have you here, Lynn. We appreciate your taking care of that little munchkin during the wedding."

So far, no one had shown any hint of recognition. Lynn's shoulders relaxed a little. "I'm happy to." She shifted some of the baby's light hair out of her eyes and secured it behind her ear. "Congratulations to the both of you."

Chess looped an arm around Brooke's waist and kissed her soundly on the lips. Brooke looked at him lovingly as she tucked herself into his shoulder.

Nathan returned with the other two people there. "And this is Joel and Anna. Guys, this is Lynn."

Lynn shook each of their hands. Between the wedding bands they both wore, and the way Joel was holding Anna's hand in his, it was clear they were married.

It would seem Lynn and Nathan were the only single adults in the group. Nice.

Lynn cleared her throat, thankful for the distraction of Mia in her arms. "So everyone's in the wedding party?"

Chess nodded. "Nathan's my best man, and Anna is Brooke's maid of honor."

"And Joel," Brooke began, "will be giving me away." She

smiled before turning for the back door. "I'm going to go see if everything else is ready."

"I'll help," Anna said and disappeared after her.

Chess pointed to the grill. "It shouldn't be long before we're ready to eat. I'll go check on the steaks."

Lynn looked from Nathan to Joel and back. Should she offer to go inside and help the other women? Mia laid her head on Lynn's shoulder as though she had nowhere else in the world she'd rather be. Lynn's heart turned over in her chest.

"You're right," Joel said. "Mia will be just fine with Lynn."

Lynn patted the baby's back. "So how do you two know each other?"

"That's a long story." Joel exchanged a look with Nathan that Lynn couldn't quite read. "I consider Chess and Brooke to be my brother and sister by choice. And this guy," he jabbed a thumb at Nathan, "was the buy two, get one free."

Nathan gave Joel a good natured shove and laughed. He reached for Mia. "I'm going to go change this girl's diaper before it's time to eat." He tossed Lynn a smile. "You do enough of that during the week. Grab a seat and relax."

With that, he was gone.

Lynn awkwardly slipped her hands into her pockets. Joel moved a lawn chair forward a bit and motioned to it before sitting down in another one. Lynn joined him.

"This is a great place. The backyard is amazing."

Joel nodded. "We all lived in Quintin until this last October. Brooke got an apartment a few blocks from here. Once she and Chess became engaged, they found this house. Now he lives here and once they're married, she'll move in and let the apartment go."

"That's awesome. And you and Anna plan to stay in Quintin?"

"We do. We own a diner there." Joel looked up when the back door opened and both women came back through with bowls of mashed potatoes and corn, and a pitcher with gravy.

"Perfect timing." Chess approached with a platter full of steaks. "I was thinking we could eat out here if there are no objections."

Everyone placed food on the large picnic table nearby. Despite her nerves, Lynn's stomach growled. "Everything looks great." She glanced at the door as Nathan and Mia appeared. Nathan gave his daughter a kiss on the head that had Lynn suppressing a sigh. When Nathan put a hand to her back and escorted her to the table, finally taking a seat next to her, Lynn's pulse went into overdrive. She grasped the glass of ice water in hopes the cool surface would keep her emotions from painting themselves all over her face.

NATHAN PASSED the corn to Lynn. Conversation around the table was just as spirited as it always was when the gang got together for dinner. Still, Lynn seemed unusually quiet. She smiled and answered questions when asked directly, but she never really jumped in on her own. He wondered if she was always this shy and found himself curious as to what topics would inspire her to speak up more.

He used a spoon to try and control the amount of mashed potatoes on his young daughter's face but quickly gave up. "Chess, I'm going to have to borrow your bathtub to clean this kiddo up before I can head home."

That brought a round of laughter as Mia fisted more

mashed potatoes and put them into her mouth, completely oblivious to the attention of the adults around her.

Brooke addressed Lynn from the other side of the table. "How long have you worked at the daycare, Lynn?"

Lynn wiped her hands off on a napkin before answering. "Right at two years." She smiled at Mia. "It keeps me on my toes."

"I can imagine." Chess took a drink of his soda. "We watch my niece one day a week, and she about wears us out."

When Nathan kicked him under the table, Chess laughed. "I'm kidding. I wish we had a way to keep her more often." His eyes softened as he looked at Mia. "Seriously, though, hats off to anyone who can wrangle a whole room full of kids and live to tell the tale."

Lynn shrugged. "I grew up helping with my little sister and volunteering in the nursery at church."

That sentence snagged Nathan's attention. If Lynn grew up in church, was she still religious? While Nathan didn't go to church nearly as often as he should, there was no doubt how often God had guided his life. He was also surprised by the news that she had family. He'd had the impression she was on her own. "Where does your sister live?"

Lynn's smile fell, but she tried to hide it by reaching for her drink. "I'm not really in touch with my family anymore." There was a hint of sadness in her voice. To Lynn's credit, she pulled herself together, managed another smile, and changed the subject. "I thought I'd drive by the church on my way home. After Nathan told me where it was, I looked it up online. It's beautiful."

Her segue was effective and had the ladies talking about wedding details for the remainder of the meal. Her ability to skirt around the question had Nathan curious about her family and her past. There was a lot he didn't know about Lynn, and it surprised him how much he'd like to change that.

Lynn was the first woman he'd been interested in since Mia's mother, and he wasn't entirely sure whether he wanted to acknowledge it or not. Pushing those thoughts from his mind, he focused on visiting with everyone. After a while they all had dessert, and then people started to go their separate ways.

Brooke offered to give Mia a bath. Nathan handed her over and then walked Lynn out to her car.

"I'm glad you came. I think Mia was excited to see you. She'll do just fine with you at the wedding."

Lynn nodded. "I think it'll work out, too." She tilted her head toward the house. "Your family seems great. I had no idea you'd only just met your brother last year." Her voice was thick with curiosity, but to her credit, she didn't push with more questions.

Nathan never minded sharing how things had worked out. "Chess pretty much took care of me when I was a baby. When I was three—and he was eight—we entered the foster care system. It's a long story, but a couple adopted me, and Chess and I got separated. I was too young to search for him, and he had no idea about the adoption, so it took a while for us to find each other again. But once we did, I didn't hesitate to move up here so we could be closer to family."

"Wow, it sounds like something straight out of a movie. I'm glad you guys reconnected again."

"Me, too." He paused, watching her closely. "So what's up with your family? Why aren't you in touch?" Yeah, he was being pushy. And the guarded look in her eyes told him she wasn't likely to open up to him. Not now, anyway.

Lynn gave a subtle shrug. "Let's just say I'm a huge disappointment. The one thing my father didn't want me to pursue in life was my dream. I chose to follow that, and it left me all but disowned. And my sister…" Moisture gathered in her eyes. "She has Down syndrome along with some other special needs and still lives with them. So when I lost my parents, I lost her, too."

"I'm sorry to hear that." He couldn't imagine Lynn doing anything that would be worthy of a parent disowning her. The thought of it made him angry. He watched Lynn as she folded her arms in front of her like a shield between her and the world. His heart went out to her. "I know what it's like to be alone." He motioned to the house. "We all do. We've had periods in our lives where we didn't know if we'd ever find a family. But God brought us together." Nathan put a hand on her arm and wondered whether her skin was that warm, or if his hands were cold. "I have no doubt that He has a plan in mind for you, too."

She shrugged again. "I hope so." Lynn smiled then as her cheeks turned pink. "I really didn't mean to get into all of that. Thank you again for the invitation to join you all for dinner. I enjoyed it."

"I'm glad, so did I. I guess I'll see you on Monday?"

"I'll see you then." She raised a hand. "Bye, Nathan."

"Bye, Lynn." He watched until she'd gotten in her car and it rounded the corner.

There was something about the beguiling woman with those vulnerable hazel eyes. She needed someone, and heaven help him, he wanted to be there for her.

"Alright, God. I have no idea if this is just me potentially making a mess of things, or if some of this is Your idea." Either way, he was glad he'd asked Lynn to care for Mia during the wedding. Truth be told, he'd enjoyed spending extra time with her and was already looking forward to seeing her again on Monday.

4

L ynn spent the rest of the weekend thinking about her dinner with Nathan's family. By the time Monday morning came around, she had no idea what to expect from Nathan. Would he act like he normally did, as though she hadn't had dinner with him at all? Or would things be different? Did she want things to be different?

Even Lynn knew she was way overthinking everything. But she couldn't help the way her heart hiccupped when Nathan came in with Mia on Monday. He waved at her with a smile, signed in, and then lifted Mia up.

"She smells a lot better today than she did last time." His blue eyes sparkled with humor.

Mia reached for Lynn, and she took the baby. "Yes, she does." Lynn chuckled. "Thank you again for inviting me on Saturday. It was a relief knowing that Mia won't freak out on me when I show up at the church."

"Truthfully? I think she's just as comfortable with you as she is with Chess, Brooke, and the others."

Something flashed across Nathan's face, but Lynn couldn't quite decipher its meaning before it'd disappeared.

Nathan studied Lynn for a moment before shifting his gaze back to his daughter. "You be good for Miss Lynn. I'll see you in a while." He kissed the baby's cheek and smiled. "Thanks, Lynn. I hope you both have a great day."

"You, too, Nathan."

With one last look behind him, Nathan left the daycare center.

"It's you and me, bug." Lynn cuddled Mia close and took her into the nursery. "You ready to go play?"

The day went smoothly. That evening, Nathan picked Mia up, Lynn helped Sharon disinfect toys, then it was time to go home.

While Lynn tried not to eat out too often, she reserved Monday evenings for such a treat. After debating her choice of food, she finally pulled into the parking lot of one of the burger joints in town. It was more fast food than anything, but their bacon cheeseburger was calling.

Determined to go in instead of using the drive through, which was well known for its slow progress this time of day, Lynn parked and entered the busy building. She placed her order, including a chocolate milkshake, and then stood to the side to wait for her name to be called. Only then did she allow her gaze to roam the interior of the burger joint. That's when she spotted Nathan and Mia sitting at a table on the other side of the dining area.

Nathan looked up at that moment and saw her. Surprise showed on his face followed by a smile. He waved.

Lynn returned the gesture at the same time that someone at the counter called her name.

She picked up the bag of food along with her shake. She couldn't really leave without saying hello, so she changed course and headed for Nathan's table. "Great minds think alike, I see."

"Yes, but don't tell Joel we're eating here. He and Anna own a crazy good burger joint in Quintin, and this is, by far, a distant second to that. But you do what you gotta do."

Lynn enjoyed the way humor caused the corners of Nathan's eyes to crinkle. She smiled in return. "My lips are sealed."

Nathan pointed to her bag. "You should join us."

Lynn hadn't expected the invitation. She'd come over because she didn't want to seem rude just waving and leaving. Well, and talking to Nathan was certainly a bonus. But join them? As had become a habit, she glanced around the restaurant as though someone might recognize her.

Nathan chuckled. "You have to eat it, you may as well sit down here."

The genuine look of welcome on his face combined with Mia's happy mood made up Lynn's mind. She finally nodded once and took the chair opposite Nathan. "Thank you." She unpacked her food and set it out on the table. After taking a drink of her thick milkshake, she sighed approvingly. "Chocolate milkshake. People can say what they will about this place, but their milkshakes are awesome."

"They are good. But you'll have to go to Quintin and have one from J's Parkview Diner. Joel's strawberry milkshakes are made with fresh strawberries. Then he makes seasonal shakes as well, like peach or blackberry." Nathan dipped a fry into ketchup and put it in his mouth.

"A fresh peach milkshake? I will have to give that a try."

"Maybe Mia and I can take you one of these days."

Lynn had been about to take a bite of her bacon cheeseburger but his words froze her motions. She glanced at him, and he seemed as surprised at his own words as she was. Was he asking her out on a date? Was it a casual get together? Or was he just being polite and now he was worried she'd take him up on the offer?

She took a bite to prolong her response time. Any hope that she might come up with the right thing to say disappeared by the time she'd finished it. Lynn was still mulling over her response when Nathan seemed to take pity on her.

"I didn't mean to make you uncomfortable." Nathan broke two French fries into bite-sized pieces for Mia. "If it helps, I made myself uncomfortable in the process."

Lynn looked up to find him watching her, the truth of his statement in his eyes. He chuckled, and she joined him. "Sorry." She shrugged. "I tend to second-guess myself and what other people mean. I've not had the best luck with guys in the past." That was more than she should've said, but it was out there now.

"Trust me, I get that. My track record with women isn't great, either." He used a napkin to wipe some ketchup off Mia's chin. "Mia's mother and I broke up. At the time, I thought it was the worst thing that could happen to me. But then we found out about Mia. When Gwen told me she didn't want a baby, I realized what the worst thing really would be."

Lynn had wondered often what happened to Mia's mother. Now that Nathan was telling her, she didn't know what to say. "I'm sorry. I can only imagine how difficult that was."

Nathan nodded. "I convinced her to carry the baby to term for monetary support and then she signed away all parental rights to Mia." He placed a hand on his daughter's head lovingly. "It's just been the two of us. Or it was, until I found Chess. Now we have a family."

"A true answer to prayer." The wistful tone of her own voice surprised even her. She felt Nathan's eyes on her.

He cleared his throat. "Look, I know what it's like to do things on your own. And what it's like to have family walk away." He paused. "I also know what a difference good friends can make. I think there's always room for another friend in our lives, don't you?"

Lynn's chest expanded as his words settled over her heart. "Yes, there's always room for another friend."

"Good." Nathan smiled. "So maybe taking you to Quintin is a too big of first step in our new friendship. What about breakfast on Saturday before I go to work?"

That was the second time Nathan had mentioned working on the weekend. "What kind of work do you do?"

"I'm an instructor at a Brazilian jiu-jitsu academy here in town."

Well, Lynn wouldn't have guessed that one. Her face must have said the same because Nathan laughed.

"I get that response a lot."

"Do you teach kids? Or adults?"

Nathan took a drink of his soda. "All of the above."

"What got you into that line of work?" Lynn set her burger down and gave Nathan her full attention. She tried to picture him doing fancy moves like she'd seen on The Karate Kid and failed.

NATHAN HELPED Mia take a drink of apple juice as he mulled his response to Lynn's question. His daughter wasn't quite able to hold the juice box without wearing half of the contents.

"Honestly? I was an angry kid. My adoptive parents got a divorce when I was ten and lived separate lives. I bounced back and forth all the time. They told each other lies as naturally as breathing. I shouldn't have been surprised to find out they'd lied to me, too. They probably thought they were protecting me, but they originally told me that my big brother didn't want to be adopted and that's why they only adopted me. I later found out that they just didn't want to adopt two kids and left Chess behind."

"Wow, that's horrible. I'm sorry, Nathan." Lynn frowned.

"Well, I'm sure I was a difficult kid to handle, too. I got into a lot of fights in school. One of my teachers really got to me when I was sixteen, and I tried to punch him. He could've punished me or even had me suspended. Instead, he convinced my dad to enroll me in a Brazilian jiu-jitsu class. Honestly, it was the best thing anyone ever did for me." Nathan thought back on how he used to act. His life could have turned out badly if it weren't for that teacher who took the time to make a difference. "It turned out I had a lot of anger I needed to work out. My instructor there stuck with me, and he's the one who gave me a referral to the job here."

Her burger forgotten, Lynn leaned back in her chair and shook her head in amazement. "I guess it goes to show how much of a difference one person can make in someone else's life. I'm glad you had that."

"Me, too." Mia had finished eating and was beginning to fidget. Nathan pushed his chair away from the table and lifted her out of the highchair before settling her in his lap. "You never did answer my question, though. About breakfast on Saturday." He grinned when she blinked at him, and her cheeks turned pink. "You know, if you decide to wear some comfortable clothes, you could always come to the academy and try out a free class afterward."

"I think you'd end up regretting that offer if I showed up."

"I'm pretty sure I wouldn't." He raised an eyebrow in challenge. He watched her face as he waited for a response, all the while hoping she'd agree.

"Breakfast, huh?"

Nathan flashed her a grin. "I'm buying."

Lynn chuckled then as she brushed some hair away from her face. "Okay. Breakfast on Saturday sounds great."

"Awesome. And the class?"

"The jury's still out on that one." Lynn smiled.

"That's okay. I have five days to change your mind."

JEB HAD GONE through his social media routine every night for more nights than he dared to count. At this moment, he was performing the usual searches while watching a show stream on television and eating a frozen dinner straight from the microwave.

He finally looked up from a particularly funny part of the show and stopped as his eyes scanned the computer screen.

Someone had shared a picture along with the post, "I may have just seen Bethany Truitt eating at a burger joint in Fort Worth." The photo itself was terrible. It was taken from what appeared to be the drive-through and the reflections on the restaurant window made it nearly impossible to tell the person in question was even a woman.

Jeb still marked the information down in his notebook, did a specific search for Bethany in Fort Worth, and then leaned back in his chair.

He'd traveled on a less detailed possibility.

A memory nagged at him from the back of his mind. Wasn't there an interview with Bethany back when her group first formed where she said she was from Texas?

The possibility of a connection had him setting his meal aside and leafing through one of his notebooks dedicated to all things Bethany. If he could just find that reference, he might be able to…

Aha! Not only had he written down that little detail, but he'd written the date of the interview.

Giddy with excitement, he searched online until he located a copy. Hands shaking, he started the video clip. Jeb had forgotten how much more she smiled back then compared to the interviews toward the end of her career.

Oh, there it is. He turned the volume up and leaned closer.

The reporter conducting the interview smiled. "So what's it like to travel from town to town on tour?"

Bethany chuckled. "I have to admit, it's taking a lot of getting used to. I'm just a small-town Texas girl. I'm not used to all of this."

Jeb rewound the video and listened to her response three times before letting the interview finish.

Fort Worth was anything but a small town. That said, if she used to live in Texas, maybe that's where she went back to when she quit performing. There could be any number of reasons why she chose to move to Fort Worth.

It was one of the best leads he'd had in a long, long time.

Still, the last time he took off, he'd nearly lost his job. He couldn't risk that without more proof that Bethany might be there. For now, he'd wait and watch social media. If someone truly saw her, then another sighting was bound to occur.

He snatched up his meal, stuck it back in the microwave, and leaned against the counter with satisfaction.

"Bethany, I will find you again."

5

Throughout the week, Nathan looked forward to the small moments when he visited with Lynn at the daycare center. By the time Saturday morning came around, they'd decided to meet at seven at one of the waffle houses in town. When he told Chess about it, Chess and Brooke immediately offered to take Mia in a little earlier so that Nathan could meet Lynn without the baby. Chess couldn't do it without a great deal of ribbing, but Nathan ignored it.

Honestly, it felt weird not to have Mia in his arms as he got out of his Jeep and walked to the front of the waffle house. Lynn must have thought so, too, because she looked at him quizzically when he found her waiting for him inside.

"You forget someone?" The teasing expression on her face brought out a smile of his own.

Nathan took in her cotton pants and comfortable-looking shirt. He hoped this meant she might try out a class, but thought he'd hold off mentioning anything for now. "I went ahead and took Mia by Chess's place. I guess Brooke's making muffins or something. I'm sure Mia will enjoy it. She likes to 'help'

Brooke bake. I'm quite certain it makes the whole process about four times harder, but Brooke doesn't seem to mind." Nathan escorted her to an empty table. "Have you eaten here before?"

"A time or two. Their blueberry waffles are to die for." Lynn shook out a napkin and placed it in her lap. She glanced around the dining area several times before looking at him again.

"Those are good, though I'm partial to the cream cheese stuffed French toast." A waitress stopped by their table and took their drink orders.

Lynn asked for a glass of orange juice. When they were alone again, she smiled. "It's nice that Brooke enjoys baking."

"I think we all enjoy it, too." Nathan laughed, remembering all of the desserts and other goodies Brooke had shared with him in the last six months. "Do you like to bake?"

Lynn had just taken a sip of her water and had to put her napkin in front of her mouth to keep from spitting it out. Once she'd swallowed she laughed. "Oh, no. Me and baking don't get along. In fact, I avoid it at all costs. As you could tell by my incredibly fancy brownies that I brought by last weekend."

Nathan just assumed she'd been in a hurry and hadn't thought much of it. "Brownies are good no matter where they come from. So what are your hobbies? What do you like to do when you aren't taking care of kids?"

She hesitated a moment, which seemed a little odd. Most people had no problem talking about their hobbies. She glanced around them as though looking for someone before answering. "I like music."

"Listening or playing? What type?"

"I'll listen to just about anything. I've got pretty eclectic tastes. I prefer to play pop or rock."

That surprised him. "You play an instrument?"

Lynn pulled her cell phone out and checked the screen. With her eyes on it, she nodded. "Piano. But it's been a little while." She slipped it back into her pocket. "What about you? What are your hobbies?"

"I guess martial arts qualifies as both that and my job. I teach at the academy six days a week, mostly for the extra money, but partly because I like helping people see the strength they didn't know they had. When I'm not working, I spend most of my time with Mia and our family." He shrugged. "Now that I'm saying it, maybe it's pathetic I don't really have other things I focus on."

"I don't think so." Lynn looked up as the waiter arrived with their juices. She took a tentative sip of hers and nodded appreciatively. "Outside of music, I don't have a whole lot, either. I just got a cat. Or rather, he found me. But I don't think that really counts."

Nathan had always admired people who played an instrument—especially those who played one well. He wanted to ask her more about it, but the moment had passed. Instead, he asked her about the cat and then couldn't stop laughing after she shared how she met the cat in the first place. Just when he got control of his amusement, he tried to picture her sneaking through the kitchen with a rolling pin in her hand, and he was laughing again.

Lynn's eyes sparkled. "Oh, I know. Seriously, it's too bad I didn't have a video of it. I could probably win some money somewhere." She shrugged. "I'm not kidding, though. That rolling pin is heavy enough to knock out a horse."

He cleared his throat and took a drink of water. "See, there's another reason why you should come by for a free class later this morning. Then you'll be able to protect yourself and your new cat without the use of a rolling pin."

Their food arrived at that moment, interrupting any reply Lynn might have given him. He accepted his plate of stuffed French toast. "And it's a good thing I have nearly two hours before my first class or those students will have to teach themselves after I eat this." There was way more food on his plate than he was going to be able to eat. But then again, that was the case no matter what you ordered at this restaurant.

Lynn's platter of waffles looked like enough for two adults. She didn't waste any time adding blueberry syrup to the blueberry-topped waffles. "Now that looks amazing. You know, this is the only place I can find now that has blueberry syrup. I remember pancake houses had it all the time when I was a kid."

When he was young, Nathan never ate at restaurants that served breakfast unless it was a convenience store. His parents were big on cooking at home over fast food. Which was funny since they spent the meal time arguing. Just thinking about it brought a frown to his face that he quickly replaced with a smile. "Well, they have some amazing food here."

They ate in comfortable silence for a while before Lynn set her fork down and leaned back in her seat. She held her arms out to her sides. "Okay, I dressed for a class just in case, but I'm not sure I should take one. Martial arts of any kind aren't exactly something I can picture myself doing."

His French toast forgotten, Nathan leaned forward a little. "Jiu-jitsu is fun, great exercise, and a way to help build self-esteem. Besides, it's more fun if you're taking classes with a friend—even if that friend is teaching them."

"You don't give up easily, do you?"

"I do not."

"Then I guess I'll have to try one of these classes you've raved about. See if the instructor is all he's cracked up to be." She quirked an eyebrow before going back to her breakfast.

Nathan tried to focus on his food again, but all he could think about was how easy it was to talk to Lynn. Their banter was natural, and he was pretty sure he could visit with her for hours and not grow tired of it.

Getting into a relationship was the last thing he'd thought about two weeks ago. But as he watched Lynn across the table, he could picture that with her. The realization both scared and intrigued him in equal measures.

LYNN HAD DRESSED in some cotton pants that morning and a baggy tan t-shirt just in case she decided to take Nathan up on the invitation to class. Her intention was to play it by ear and see how breakfast went.

She hadn't anticipated spending nearly two hours at the waffle house eating and talking. They might have stayed longer if some of the staff wasn't giving them some funny looks. They finally took pity on them, Nathan paid the bill, and they left the restaurant.

Now she was following him through town to the academy where he promised to show her around while they waited for his first class to begin.

Butterflies flitted around in her stomach as they pulled into a parking lot and found spaces to park. It was ridiculous to be this nervous. After all, she'd performed in front of huge crowds many times in the past. This ought to be a cake-walk. Annoyed with herself, she tried to shove her nerves aside as she got out of her car.

Nathan told her about the academy and about Gregor, the

man who owned it. Lynn noted the photos of individuals and classes that covered the walls inside while shelves proudly displayed trophies.

Nathan led the way to the front counter. He leaned over and nabbed a piece of paper while the woman behind the counter spoke to someone else on the phone. She shot Nathan a smile.

He handed the paper and a pen to Lynn. "Here, if you'll fill this out, then we'll have everything we need in case you decide to come back after today."

The hopeful look on his face was adorable. It was almost enough to make Lynn commit to the class right now. "You're very optimistic."

"I try." He cupped her elbow with a large hand. "If you're good here, I need to go get a few things ready before class starts."

All Lynn could do was nod. He squeezed her elbow slightly before moving away. It took her several moments to stop thinking about the way his touch had sent her pulse into a gallop.

When she'd finished filling out the form and handed it to the woman behind the counter, Lynn turned and made her way to the mats out on the floor.

There were several families already out there. Lynn was relieved to see she wasn't the only individual to join as well.

Nathan held a clipboard and made several notes before looking up with a smile. "Good morning, everyone. I hope you all had a good week." Several murmurs followed along with one young girl who announced that she lost a tooth. Nathan knelt down to see the new gap in her mouth and nodded appreciatively. "That's awesome, Sarah."

"Now I can do this!" The little girl stuck the tip of her tongue through the gap, eliciting chuckles all around.

Nathan gave her a high five, and she went back to stand with her family. "We have two people trying out the class today. Please welcome Vince," he pointed to a guy who didn't look the least bit nervous, "and Lynn."

Lynn gave a little wave and what she hoped was a normal smile. Nathan's gaze rested on her a moment longer before he started the class.

She had no idea what to expect from jiu-jitsu, but she was surprised that the first twenty minutes of the class was comprised of stretching and conditioning exercises. It made sense, especially considering how difficult some of them were. Lynn did her best to keep up with everyone else and thought she didn't do too badly. Only once did Nathan have to stop by and help her correct her form.

Once they'd finished warming up, Nathan explained what they'd been doing last week. He called up another guy to demonstrate the hold. Lynn worried about who she would be sparring with until Nathan paired her with another woman. She ignored the one-part disappointment mixed with the three-parts relief that she wouldn't be sparring with Nathan.

Even then, Lynn felt awkward and uncoordinated as she tried to figure out the hold. At one point, Nathan came over to them.

"You're doing great, Lynn, but you need to put your arm on the other side. Like this." He placed a hand on her arm and showed her where it should be positioned.

The whole time, Lynn willed herself not to blush, although she was certain her face was already red from exertion. Her lighter complexion and the ease with which she blushed was one of the things she'd always hated growing up.

She'd since learned how to control her reactions better. Except, apparently, when she was in Nathan's presence.

With the help of her partner, she tried to follow his directions and got a nod of approval. Hopefully she wasn't making a complete fool of herself.

———

LYNN HAD CLEARLY NEVER PARTICIPATED in any form of martial arts. Nathan could tell she was trying just as hard as anyone else, though, and saw improvement in that first class. If she decided to sign up for his class, he was certain she could pick things up quickly.

He stopped to help her and Jasmine several times as they practiced holds. Every time he spoke directly to Lynn, she maintained eye contact just enough to get directions before she was focusing on the exercise or hold itself. He wasn't sure if she was that intent on his instructions, or if she was nervous around him. That last possibility intrigued him.

They finished the lesson. Once he'd answered questions from other students, he moved to speak with Lynn. "You did great out there. Are you considering signing up for next week?"

She hesitated. "I'm not sure. I thought about seeing if a friend from work might be interested in coming with me." Her cheeks reddened, and she seemed to find a worn spot on the floor particularly interesting. "Then again, I might be better off getting a taser or some pepper spray. Or maybe a nice, metal baseball bat to carry around with me."

Lynn smiled, but there was something in her eyes that hinted she might be speaking some truth. He ought to laugh at her attempt to joke, but his instincts insisted he address what she wasn't quite saying.

"Are you trying to be cautious in general? Or is there something—or someone—you feel like you need to be ready to defend yourself against?"

She shrugged and jabbed a thumb at the door. "I should probably go and let you get to your next class."

Nathan had grown up an expert at skirting around the issues right in front of him. He knew avoidance when he saw it. He reached out and touched her upper arm, effectively halting her escape. "Lynn..."

She glanced around as though afraid she might be overheard. "It's silly. There was someone, but it's been years." Her voice caught. She swallowed and took a moment before continuing. "I know I'm being neurotic. I should let it all go, but it's hard to quit looking over my shoulder."

Those very shoulders sagged a little as an air of defeat crossed her features.

He motioned to her. "Follow me." He led her to the break room. Thankfully, no one was using it currently so they had the small space to themselves. He wished he knew what had happened to Lynn in the past. Had someone hurt her? Abused her? The very thought had anger boiling in his gut. Nathan would love to see the guy walk into the building right now.

He sat on the edge of the table in the center of the room. "You don't have to tell me about it. I imagine people have insisted that you need to let go and move forward. In some ways, they're right. It's easy to let the past grab onto us and keep us from enjoying anything else that might come our way." His jiu-jitsu instructor back in the day had told him much the same thing. "At the same time, it's impossible to forget what happened. Things like that change you." Their situations were different, but he knew full well how true his words were.

Lynn seemed to relax a little and only offered him a small nod. "I hate that it changed me, but I'm not sure I can ever fully shake it."

Nathan had to make a point of not trying to imagine what

might have happened to her. Whatever it was, it had affected her completely, and saddened him. "Don't expect yourself to. Just move forward. That's all we can really do."

She nodded again and watched him for several moments. "Something tells me you're speaking from experience."

He didn't usually open up about his past, but the vulnerability in her eyes had him quickly relenting. "Let's just say I wouldn't wish my memories of my parents on my enemies. It was enough to either make you never want to have kids of your own, or swear you'll be a better parent. My brother, Chess, went the first direction until he met and fell in love with Brooke. I guess I've always felt the opposite."

"You're a great dad to Mia, Nathan. She's lucky to have you."

Her words settled over his heart like a warm blanket. "I appreciate that." Nathan glanced at his watch. "I need to get out there for my next class, but if you ever need to talk, I hope you know I'm here." He paused. "I do hope you'll invite your friend to class. It'd be great to see you both here. Two weeks from today, of course, since next Saturday is the wedding."

Lynn laughed at that, and the sound swirled around them like a beautiful strain of music. Nathan was glad to see her smiling again.

"Of course. And I'll ask her, but I won't make any promises."

"I can live with that." He winked at her as he pulled the door open again and let her go through ahead of him. "I guess I'll see you on Monday. Maybe we can manage to run into each other somewhere for dinner this week." He turned to face her just in time to see a small smile tugging at the corners of her mouth.

"Maybe so. Have a good weekend, Nathan. Thanks again for breakfast."

"Anytime."

He watched as she walked out. He was disappointed she hadn't committed to the class, but encouraged by the fact she hadn't completely shot down his suggestion of having dinner again soon.

JEB THREW some clothes into a duffel bag and zipped it up. He mentally ran through a list of the things he might need over the next week or two. Confident he had the important things packed, he tossed the duffel bag by the front door and sat at his computer again.

For the tenth time that evening, he studied the photo that had been posted to social media. There was no doubting it was Bethany. She looked like she'd gained a few pounds, but that profile—he'd know it anywhere.

Someone had spotted her at a waffle house in Fort Worth. He'd already contacted the person and sent a private message asking which waffle house it was. They still hadn't answered.

That was okay. They had time as he drove from his small place in Tennessee.

Jeb called to let his brother, who also happened to be his boss, know he'd be taking a few days off work. His brother wasn't exactly thrilled, but since Jeb owned a portion of their father's business, there wasn't a lot more that could be said.

Besides, he had more important things to think about. He'd leave for Fort Worth as soon as he finished getting ready.

A slow smile spread across his face. "Don't worry, Bethany. We'll see each other again soon."

6

"So how was it?" Sharon's eyes glittered with curiosity as she stood in a room full of moving people, patiently waiting for Lynn's response.

Lynn glanced at the crowd of churchgoers around them. Granted, they were all busy picking kids up from their classes or heading out to whatever they planned for the rest of their Sunday. They likely didn't have time to listen to whatever Lynn might tell her friend. Still...

She hooked Sharon's arm with her own and led her outside where they had more privacy. By the time they got there, Sharon was laughing. "You are such a mess. Maybe I was referring to the part of the church service when I had to step out to go to the bathroom."

"You don't really expect me to believe that, do you?" Lynn scanned the area around the church, confident that no one had noticed their presence. "Isn't your husband going to come looking for you?"

"He volunteered to help clean up today. We've got at least half an hour to visit." Sharon gave her a look that proved just how proud she was of herself. "Come on, my curiosity is killing me. What was Nathan like? How was breakfast? Did you go to one of his classes?"

Sharon's honest interest meant Lynn couldn't stay annoyed with her friend for long.

"He was a perfect gentleman. He bought my breakfast and opened up about his family." Regret collided with guilt as she thought about how kind he'd been. "And here I haven't even told him who I really am. What does that say about me?"

"It says things are complicated." Sharon's eyes softened as she looked at Lynn. "Nathan's a single dad with a little girl. It sounds like his past is pretty complicated, too. I'm betting he'd understand if you told him everything."

"Maybe. Probably." Lynn had gone through the whole scenario in her head more times than she could count. "But if he doesn't, then either he won't have someone to watch Mia at the wedding, or it's going to be really awkward between us. Waiting until afterward to tell him about everything makes the most sense."

Lynn couldn't tell whether Sharon agreed with her or not. Sharon was always one to express an opinion when she needed to, but she was also good about staying quiet and letting Lynn think through things on her own. Something Lynn always appreciated.

And she'd had a lot to think about since she last spoke with Nathan.

"Sounds like things were a mess for him growing up. Yet, here he is with a great family and a sweet daughter." She'd already shared some about the dinner with him and his family and how put together they seemed. Lynn shrugged. "I guess I'm a little in awe of how he went through all that and didn't let it completely mess up his life."

"Insinuating that you did?" Sharon was already shaking her head. "You know that's not true."

"I *know* it's not true, but I don't usually *feel* that way." The church crowd was beginning to thin a little, so Lynn led the way to a small bench underneath one of the large oak trees. The women sat down. "It sounds like Nathan looked high and low for his brother, never truly giving up on the search even years later." Tears pricked at the back of Lynn's eyelids, and she tried to blink them away. She swallowed hard against a lump forming in her throat. "I know my parents gave up on me years ago. But by no longer trying, it's as though I've given up on Perry." She pictured her little sister and that was enough to send a tear cascading down her cheek. "What kind of person does that make me? What does she think of me?"

Sharon laid her Bible down on the bench beside her. "First of all, from everything you've told me, it sounds like Perry has way too many great memories of the two of you together to allow distance to wash them away."

Lynn nodded, hoping her friend was right. She and Perry had such a fun time growing up together, and had a special bond that even her parents didn't have with Perry. Lynn hoped her sister held onto those wonderful childhood memories as much as she did.

"And secondly," Sharon nudged Lynn's arm with her own, "just because you stayed away like your father demanded doesn't mean that will always be the case. Maybe things have changed."

Lynn seriously doubted it. But maybe Sharon was right. Maybe staying away wasn't the answer anymore. She sniffled. When Sharon handed her a tissue, she discreetly blew her nose. "Do you think I should try to see Perry?" Was it possible for her to reconnect with her family? If Nathan and

Chess could form a new relationship after being separated for years, and if Chess, Brooke, and Joel could form a family of their own when they had none before, surely her own biological family had a chance.

"I wish I had an answer for you, Lynn. I don't think anything about your family situation is simple. But if you pray about it and give it some time, you'll feel led one way or another."

"Yeah." She'd wished so often throughout her life that God would've given her a road map. She could've avoided so many potholes. But then, if things hadn't happened the way they had, she wouldn't know Sharon now. Or Nathan and Mia. "Why does life have to be so complicated sometimes?"

"I sure wish I knew." Sharon put an arm around Lynn's shoulders. "Can I pray for you?"

Lynn nodded. As Sharon began to pray, asking for guidance not only with regards to Perry, but Nathan as well, Lynn allowed the tears to fall.

Even if God didn't hand out road maps, at least He'd never failed to travel life's paths with her. Things would work themselves out—they had to.

WHAT MADE Lynn think this was a good idea? She mentally grasped for the peace she'd felt after Sharon prayed for her yesterday.

But now it was Monday, and the further the day progressed, the more nervous she was about her decision to drive to her parents' house. She'd nearly backed out. After all, no one but Sharon even knew she was going to go. But Lynn knew that the moment she let the opportunity pass her by, she'd regret it.

Monday evening probably wasn't the best time to drive the hour and a half each way. But once her decision was made, she knew that prolonging the implementation of her plan would only mean ample time to change her mind. She needed to do this now.

As the minutes and the miles ticked by, she wondered what her parents would think. They hadn't welcomed her attempts to go home before. What made this any different? She could only hope and pray that the last two years had changed them as much as they had changed her.

Lynn intentionally loosened her grip on the steering wheel allowing blood to flow back into her knuckles. "I have no idea what I'm even supposed to say to them," she prayed. "Please give me the words. And please soften their hearts. I've already missed so much in Perry's life, I don't want to miss any more."

Would Perry be excited to see her? Or had it been so long that Lynn's little sister would take on her bashful demeanor?

The thought of Perry not wanting to give her a hug had Lynn fighting back tears.

This was definitely a horrible idea. The last thing she needed was to have to drive back home, in the dark, while crying. No, it was too late to turn back now.

She'd always wonder if her parents would've turned her away again. Wonder if they wouldn't have and she'd missed her chance to talk to her sister again. Lynn could imagine an amazing reunion with Perry, but she couldn't imagine reconnecting with her parents. Oh sure, miracles could happen. But it would take just that—a miracle.

No, she couldn't do this to herself. She couldn't allow herself to conjure up all the negative ways this little trip could go. She had to stay positive that this was the right first step to take, no matter what happened.

She turned onto a side street and stopped her car along the curb. The two-story house at the end of the cul-de-sac looked exactly like it had the last time Lynn saw it, except the trees out front seemed a little taller. She'd expected the place to look different somehow. As though the stress of the last two years ought to be evident on the house itself.

The cell phone on the passenger seat pinged making Lynn jump and sending her heart rate through the roof. She released a lungful of air as she swiped at the screen. Nathan's name appeared along with a short text. "How's your evening going?"

Lynn smiled. He had no idea how much of a loaded question that was. She almost typed back "It's fine," but stopped herself. "I'm sitting outside my mom and dad's house trying to get the courage to go knock on the door."

She didn't have to wait long for a reply.

"Wow. That's a big move. I'll be praying it goes well."

His words added a small dose of peace she needed to her mix of nerves. Knowing he was praying for her meant a lot, and suddenly she was glad she'd told him about it. It made her feel a little less alone. She responded to his text. "I appreciate that."

"Let me know how it goes if you're up to it."

His typed words made her smile. "I will. Thanks again." She slipped the phone into a small bag she'd brought with her. Sitting out here in the car for a while longer wasn't going to change her situation. She may as well go in and get this over with. Wondering what was going to happen had to be way worse than what she was going to experience. Right?

As she walked toward the house, her stomach did a flip. There was a time when approaching this place meant home. Security. Love.

Now, only a healthy dose of apprehension followed her

up the walkway to the front door. Lynn took a tentative breath. Held it.

Perry used to hate the sound of the doorbell. Lynn didn't want to risk scaring her sister if that was still the case, so she used the metal knocker to announce her presence instead.

Several excruciatingly slow moments passed until she heard the sound of approaching footsteps. Metal brushed against metal as the deadbolt slid away and the door opened.

It'd been over two years since she'd last seen her father. Looking at him now, however, Lynn could almost believe she'd traveled through time to ten more years in the future. His dark hair that once only showed gray along the temples was now more salt than pepper. She focused on his eyes. New wrinkles had taken residence at the corners, but the dark brown irises were the same.

The surprise on his face was quickly replaced with the stoic sternness she'd grown accustomed to as a child. Any hope she'd had that tonight might be different was quickly extinguished. She did her best not to let the disappointment show. "Hi, Dad." She forced herself to offer a tentative smile.

Lynn was a grown woman. Yet standing here in front of her father made her feel very much like that awkward teen who'd disappointed him over and over again.

He watched her for several heart beats before finally speaking. "Remind me: what are you calling yourself again?"

She suppressed a sigh. When she'd walked away from the music scene and changed her name, she'd told her family. At the time, she'd hoped they'd see she was serious about things being different. Instead, they'd seen it as further evidence that she was leaving her family behind. She never could do anything right. "I go by Lynn now, Dad."

"Right." He still hadn't given her any indication that he

was going to invite her into the house. "Was there something you needed? If it's money…"

"No, Dad. I don't need money." Lynn swallowed hard. "I just miss you all and was hoping I could come in and visit for a while."

He was shaking his head before the words were even out of her mouth. "It's late. Perry has an appointment with the cardiologist first thing in the morning. She needs her sleep." He shifted his hand to the doorknob as though he were ready to close the door right then.

The cardiologist? Many individuals with Down syndrome had trouble with their hearts, but thankfully, Perry hadn't been one of them. That she was needing to see a cardiologist now had Lynn worried. "Is she okay? What's going on?"

"It's only a precaution. You should go before it gets any later." Before he could shut the door, the sound of Mom's voice floated over his shoulder. "Ralph, who is it?"

Tears that were all too familiar filled Lynn's eyes as Mom came into view. Her long, blonde hair was cut short and had a lot of white in it. It was still just as pretty as ever, though. There was a time when Lynn had wished she had hair like her mom's. She looked into the eyes that were the same color as her own. "I was hoping to visit with you all for a while."

Mom took a step forward and stopped. Moisture gathered in her eyes at the same time the muscles in her jaw worked as she clenched her teeth. Sometimes Lynn thought she might be able to get through to Mom, but Mom was never one to stand against Dad, and he was an immovable force.

Mom put a hand on Dad's arm. "Like your father said, tonight isn't a good time."

"What if I came back this weekend? Could I buy you all dinner?"

There was the slightest hint of hope in Mom's eyes that

disappeared when Dad shook his head. "It's not a good idea. It's late, and you should get going before it's too dark to drive. Goodbye...Lynn."

With that, he closed the door in her face and flipped the porch light off.

Lynn had told herself that she'd be okay no matter what happened. But it was all a lie. Dad's rejection hit her with the force of a hammer, pushing her shoulders down and building pressure in her chest until it hurt. She turned away from the house and headed back to her car. When she reached it, she allowed herself one last look at the house.

That's when she saw Perry standing in a living room window. Her beautiful cherub face stared curiously. Oh, how Lynn missed her. Missed the hours spent laughing together and reading. Perry used to love it when Lynn painted her finger nails or brushed her hair.

Pangs of regret and pain had Lynn grasping for control of her emotions. She raised a hand and waved. Perry smiled and waved back before the curtain was closed again and all Lynn could see were shadows.

While Lynn had a strong need to curl up in a corner somewhere and cry, at least the trip hadn't been for nothing. At least Perry knew that Lynn had tried.

It wasn't until she was safely inside her car again that she realized tears were flowing. She swiped at her cheeks. Stupid. She ought to be used to this by now. Seeing Perry had been worth it, though. Instead of the usual helplessness she felt after speaking with her family, there was the slightest glimmer of hope.

She sniffed again and pulled her phone from her bag to text Nathan. "Thanks for the prayers. I saw my sister briefly for the first time in years."

It wasn't long before a response came through. "I'm glad. That was a fast visit."

"I wasn't exactly welcomed by my parents. Heading home now."

Lynn had just set the phone on the passenger seat and was about to shift the car into drive when her phone pinged again. "If you need to talk, feel free to call. Mia's asleep, and I'll be up for a while."

Lynn couldn't believe how tempting the offer was. But she'd told him so little about her past life or her identity. He had no clue what had alienated her from her family.

She needed to tell him—even wanted to. Tonight wasn't the right time, though. Not with the wedding just a few days away. Feeling horrible for again deflecting away from details about her own life, she responded, "I shouldn't. I think I need to crank the music and focus on getting home. Will see you tomorrow." Her guilt only increased as she sent the message.

"Okay. Be safe."

With a long drive ahead of her, and the pain of the truncated visit still fresh, she did need someone to talk to. Preferably someone who wasn't small, covered in fur, and whose only advice was, "Meow!" She might have called Sharon if she weren't worried she'd end up crying again, which certainly wouldn't make driving back to her place any easier.

Lynn focused on Perry's smile, and Nathan's kindness, as she pulled away from the curb and once again watched her childhood home disappear in the rearview mirror.

7

Nathan had a hard time wrapping his mind around what happened to Lynn last night. How did parents who hadn't seen their daughter in years find her on their front steps and still turn her away? There was a lot about the situation he didn't know. He wanted to ask her questions when he dropped Mia off at daycare this morning. She was clearly reluctant to tell him more about the situation than she already had, and Little Lambs certainly wasn't the place for him to push the issue.

His heart hurt for Lynn and the grief she must be experiencing right now.

Nathan taught his classes throughout the morning, took two different calls from Chess with questions regarding the wedding this Saturday, and was finally sitting down to lunch. He'd just warmed up his leftovers when Lynn's name flashed across his phone.

He swiped to answer. "Hey, Lynn." His first thought was Mia. The last time Lynn called him during the work day, Mia had fallen and gotten a large goose egg on her forehead. Unsure of what to do at the time, Nathan had rushed his daughter to the pediatrician where she was deemed fine. It'd taken several days before he stopped cringing every time Mia fell.

"Hi, Nathan. I'm sorry to bother you. Mia isn't feeling well. At first, I thought maybe she was just tired and ready for an early nap. She fell asleep quickly, but when she woke up, she felt warm. I've checked her temperature twice, and it's at 101.2." The sounds of Mia crying floated in from the background. "There seems to be very little I can do to comfort her right now."

The daycare center's guidelines were that, if a child had a temperature over 100.4, he or she had to stay home. So based on that alone, Nathan needed to go and pick Mia up.

"It may take me a half hour or so. I need to arrange for someone to take over my classes this afternoon. But I'll be there to get Mia as quick as I can." He secured a lid on his leftovers and shoved the container back into his lunch bag. "Thanks for calling, Lynn."

"You're welcome. We'll see you in a bit."

Nathan had no trouble getting someone to cover his classes and was on his way to Little Lambs shortly. Once inside, he signed Mia out at the front desk and made his way to the nursery area.

Before he entered, a soft rendition of "Somewhere Over the Rainbow" made its way to his ears. He didn't have to see the owner of the voice to know it was Lynn. Somehow, it didn't surprise him in the least to learn that she had the voice of an angel.

As he rounded the corner, he spotted Lynn in a rocking chair, Mia in her arms. His normally rambunctious daughter was lying quietly, her eyes on Lynn's face as the song concluded with one long, perfect note.

Lynn lifted Mia's little hand, kissed her fingers, and

smiled down at her. Anyone walking in right now might think they were mother and daughter the way they were wrapped up in each other.

Only then did Lynn glance over and notice him standing there. Her cheeks turned a pretty shade of pink. "Look, Mia. It's your daddy."

Mia sat up on Lynn's lap. She smiled at Nathan, but her eyes looked tired and her face red. He lifted her into his arms. The extra heat from her body radiated into his. "Hey, sweetheart. I'm sorry you're not feeling well. Let's get you home, take some medicine, and see if we can bring your fever down a little."

She leaned into his chest and released a tiny sigh, capturing Nathan's heart completely. He wrapped his arms around her protectively.

Lynn rose from the rocking chair. "Let me grab her bag and I'll walk out with you." Without waiting for him to respond, she retrieved it and they left the building together. "She's so glad you're here. What you saw was the rare few minutes she wasn't crying all day, unless she was asleep." She reached over and patted Mia's back.

"I'm pretty sure you could calm a grizzly bear with your singing talents." The moment the words were out of his mouth, Nathan realized it sounded like he was flirting. He almost apologized and realized he wasn't the least bit sorry. Especially when her blush returned along with a pleased smile on her face.

"I'll just be praying she feels better soon."

"I appreciate that." He frowned. "With just a few days until the wedding, I need her feeling better, and I need both of us to avoid getting sick, too."

Lynn chuckled. "Thankfully, being around little ones who are always getting sick has vastly improved my own immunity. I'm sure you've found the same teaching classes."

"You are right about that. Still, the timing is a little too close for comfort." They reached his Jeep. He leaned into the back seat to secure Mia. The moment he had her harness clicked in, she started to cry again. "I'd better get going. I don't think Miss Mia has much patience left."

Lynn passed him the diaper bag with a sympathetic smile. She placed a palm on his forearm. "If there's anything I can do, please let me know."

He glanced down at the physical connection that had electrical currents racing down his arm. At that moment, he was certain that only his daughter fussing in the car could pull him away from Lynn.

He lifted his gaze to her face while simultaneously covering her hand with his. "Thank you." The instinct to hold her hand—to hold *her*—was nearly overwhelming. He had a feeling that she'd fit into his arms perfectly. He imagined being able to rest his cheek on the top of her head and then mentally shook himself when he realized how much his mind was wandering.

Mia's fussing morphed into full crying mode. Nathan wasn't sure if he moved his hand first, or if Lynn had started to pull hers away. Now they stood facing each other, arms at their sides.

Since Mia couldn't return to daycare for a full twenty-four hours after being fever-free, that meant he wasn't going to be seeing Lynn tomorrow. That disappointing thought had him frowning. "I guess I'll see you on Thursday. I'll let you know how she's doing tomorrow."

Lynn nodded. "Sounds good."

Nathan gave a small wave before going around and getting into the Jeep. With a final look in Lynn's direction, he drove away. Even through poor Mia's cries, he could still hear the soothing sound of Lynn's voice singing.

———

To Lynn, it seemed weird to not have Mia there at the daycare center. She'd texted Nathan yesterday evening to see how the little girl was doing. Sadly, he responded saying Mia hadn't wanted to eat and spent most of the afternoon crying.

Lynn wondered how they got along last night. She was tempted to text him again, except it was only nine in the morning. If, by chance, he and Mia were able to sleep in, Lynn would feel horrible for waking them up. Instead, she busied herself caring for her little charges and trying to ignore Sharon's pointed looks.

She was marginally successful but could only take them so long. Baby Brian burped on her shoulder and then followed that with a long yawn. She rubbed his back as she moved the rocking chair back and forth with her foot. "Spit it out already."

Sharon's eyes widened as a look of mock innocence crossed her face.

Only after Lynn narrowed her eyes did Sharon finally cave in. "You've been walking around all day like you lost your best friend. Or your cat ran away."

"It seems weird to not have Mia here. Don't you think so, too?"

"Of course I do. But I suspect it's more than that for you." Sharon hiked her right eyebrow. "Just call him. See if you can take them dinner or something. I'm sure he'd appreciate it, and then you could get your Nathan fix for the day. It's a win-win."

Lynn released an exaggerated sigh. Sharon wasn't too far

off. Not that Lynn was going to admit it. So what if she didn't see Nathan yesterday when he'd come to pick up Mia? Or this morning when he'd normally drop her off? Was she really so pathetic that less than twenty-four hours had her distracted?

She chose to ignore the real question that kept teasing at the back of her mind: Was it bad that she was having constant thoughts about him in general? She convinced herself it was because she was worried about Mia and tried to focus on taking care of the little ones relying on her.

Instead, she hid a smile and turned the tables on her friend. "So you still think I should go back to Nathan's self-defense class?"

"Absolutely." Sharon pointed at Lynn. "It'd be good for you to get out regularly like that. The exercise is healthy. Plus, I think it would help you feel more in control of things so you're not as nervous all the time."

Lynn could've done without the reminder of her neurosis about someone recognizing her or following her around. "Then you should come to classes with me." There was something incredibly satisfying about seeing Sharon look shocked.

"Are you serious?"

"Yep. If I go, you're coming with me. I want to take the class with someone I know." She pinned her friend with a firm look. "Someone besides the instructor."

Sharon seemed to think about that for several moments. "I want to talk to Walt about it first, but I think it would be fun!"

Honestly, Lynn had expected Sharon to put up a bit of a fight. Now Lynn was going to have to go back to Nathan's class, and she'd have yet another witness to her pathetic attempts to learn jiu-jitsu. Just the thought of it had her chuckling to herself.

By the end of her work day, however, she'd thought about Sharon's suggestion and decided it was a good one. Whether Mia was doing better today or not, Nathan was probably ready for something else to eat—especially if he didn't have to fix it himself.

Sitting in her car in the parking lot, she pulled her phone out and wrote a text to Nathan. "Hey, if it's not too forward, could you send me your address? I thought I might bring dinner by for you guys."

It wasn't long before he answered her. "That would be amazing. Thank you." And he included his address.

Lynn ran by the house for a few things before heading toward the burger place. She'd noted what both he and Mia were eating when she'd first run into them there. Figuring that was probably safe, she ordered the same thing for them, and a meal for herself as well to eat after she dropped theirs off.

When she finally located Nathan's home, she pulled her car beside his in the wide driveway and retrieved the food from the back seat.

She'd barely knocked before he opened the door and ushered her inside with a tired smile. "Hey, Lynn. It's really sweet of you to do this." He closed the door behind them and cleared his throat. "Please ignore the house."

Lynn observed the living room. It was pretty cluttered, but it wasn't dirty. Clearly Nathan normally kept the house pretty clean. When her gaze rested on him, she couldn't help but notice the way the tips of his ears had turned red. He was adorable when he got embarrassed.

"Are you kidding?" Lynn laughed as Mia toddled into the room and wrapped her arms around one of Lynn's legs. "You're keeping a small, sick person alive. Your house is impressive."

"Thanks." He leaned down and scooped Mia into his arms. "Come on, you little monster. Are you hungry?"

"It looks like she's feeling better." Lynn set the bag of food on the table and watched as Nathan got Mia into her high chair. "That's great."

"Oh yes, she's feeling better. She hasn't had a fever since late last night. Unfortunately, I was up every hour checking her temperature, so I didn't get much sleep. And she's been up all day because apparently sleeping well last night means naps are unnecessary." He yawned, a hand over his mouth. "Sorry."

Smiling, Lynn shook her head. "You have nothing to apologize for." She laughed as Mia tried to grab the bag of food. Lynn started pulling things out for them and setting them on the table.

Nathan blinked. "You ought to join us." He glanced in the bag. "Did you not get anything for yourself?"

"I did. I left it out in the car. I figured I would eat later when I got home." She hadn't expected to be at Nathan's place long.

"I don't blame you if you'd rather get home after working and all. But if you're so inclined, you are welcome to bring your food inside and eat with us." The hope on his face was more than a little endearing.

Besides, she'd forgotten another small bag in her car that she'd intended to bring in. No matter which way she decided, it was going to be a little awkward. She finally gave a nod. "Okay. I'll be right back."

Nathan smiled with satisfaction and started to get Mia's food ready.

Minutes later, Lynn was back with hers and a small bag that she handed to Nathan.

"What's this?" When she nodded toward the bag, he

opened it and pulled out the box of vitamin C powder and a package of chocolate chip cookies. "What're these for?"

"The cookies are because chocolate makes everything better. The vitamin C is so you can hopefully keep from getting sick, too, with your brother's wedding just a couple days away. Trust me, I'm taking it daily myself right now for the same reason." She leaned across the table and tapped Mia's nose with a finger. "These little people can be quite the germ harborers."

That had Nathan laughing. "That's the truth. Thank you, Lynn. We will have to open the cookies after we eat." He gave her a wink.

They settled into easy conversation as they ate, mostly talking about weather, how several of the other kids at the daycare center had been out sick, and who Nathan had gotten to cover his classes.

"Have you asked your friend about coming to class a week from Saturday?" Nathan popped one more fry in his mouth before starting to clean up his wrappers.

"You must be psychic. I just did this afternoon. Sharon needs to double check her schedule and make sure her husband doesn't mind, but she thinks it would be fun to go together." Lynn willed herself to not blush when he smiled and clapped his hands together.

"That's great! It's always more fun to take classes with someone else. Is Sharon the lady at Little Lambs with the short, curly dark hair?"

Lynn nodded.

"She seems really nice. Has she and her husband been married long?"

They chatted about random things for several more minutes while she and Mia finished their dinner. By then, Mia had ketchup on her hands and even more around her mouth.

At the same time, Nathan had covered more yawns than Lynn could count. It was barely six o'clock. He probably had another hour or two before he could get Mia to bed.

A thought came to mind, and she voiced it before taking the time to talk herself out of it.

"Why don't you let me clean this up, give Mia a bath, and then we'll play for a while. You can go take a much-needed nap."

He immediately started shaking his head. "I couldn't ask you to do that. You spent all day taking care of kids. I'm sure you're more than ready to get home and rest yourself."

She might have been when she left Little Lambs. But right now, seeing Nathan so sleepy and drained, had her heart aching for him. No, she'd much rather help out here if she could. Besides, if he didn't get rest, he was more likely to get sick. She pointed that out as she stood to extricate Mia from her high chair. "I've got this. Truly. Besides, Mia's different." The moment she said that, she realized it could mean so many things.

If Nathan was wondering about it, he didn't give any indication. At first he looked as though he might argue, but apparently the need for sleep overrode his objections. "Only if you're sure. Because you're right, I can't afford to get sick. I'm going to set my alarm for an hour from now. If you need me before, just holler."

"You should try to sleep for an hour and a half," Lynn suggested. "Mia and I will have fun. Won't we, bug?"

He nodded his agreement. "Thanks, Lynn."

"No problem. See you in a bit." She watched as he retreated from the kitchen followed by the sound of a door closing.

Lynn tickled Mia's tummy. "Come on, bug. Let's see if I

can find everything we need to give you a bath. I'm pretty sure you are wearing more ketchup than you ate."

Later, as Mia splashed in a few inches of water in the bathtub, Lynn kept one hand on her as she prayed softly. "God, please help Nathan to rest well. Protect him from any illness so that he can attend his brother's wedding. Keep Mia healthy now, and if You don't mind, please keep me well, too, so I can watch Mia during the ceremony. Thank you for Your many blessings." Lynn leaned forward and kissed Mia on the top of her wet head. "Amen."

She hadn't heard a peep from Nathan. Hopefully the poor guy was sleeping peacefully. It was strange to see how she'd gone from telling Nathan she'd bring him food to caring for Mia while he slept in the other room.

Her chest tightened as she tried not to think about how much the two of them were starting to mean to her.

As NATHAN AWOKE, it took several heartbeats to understand what time it was, and why he was asleep so late in the day. The next moment, his heart jumped into his throat as Mia came to mind. He'd leaped off the bed, ready to search for her, when he remembered that Lynn had volunteered to watch her so that he could sleep.

A quick check with his phone told him the alarm was set to go off in five minutes. Wow, that hour and a half went by fast. He ran a hand over his face in hopes of wiping away the lingering fog from his nap.

He heard the muffled murmur of voices coming from the other room and followed them. In the living room, he found Lynn sitting on the floor with Mia nearby. They'd taken the set of five large, colorful blocks and were putting items of the same color on top of each.

Mia just placed a plastic orange on top of the matching block when she spotted him. She waved. "Da!"

To Nathan, it still felt like yesterday when she'd started to say his name. It never ceased to give him joy.

"Hi, Mia." He joined the girls on the floor. "Have you been good for Miss Lynn?" He turned his attention to the woman who'd gone beyond kindness to do him not one big favor, but two.

She smiled at him then, and there was something about her hanging out in his living room, playing with Mia, that made it way too easy to imagine she belonged there with them. Especially when Mia climbed into her lap and put her chubby arms around Lynn's neck. Nathan was pretty sure his heart melted into a puddle right then and there.

"She's been a sweetheart," Lynn assured him as she patted the little girl's back. "She's all cleaned up, we've done a lot of playing, and she's starting to slow down a little. With any luck, she'll be ready for bed soon and maybe you can relax a bit this evening."

The woman was seriously a miracle worker. After his nap, Nathan felt better than he had for a couple of days. "I can't thank you enough, Lynn. We both appreciate you."

"It's no problem. I was happy to help. Besides, I missed this little bug's hugs." She got to her feet, Mia still in her arms. "You be good to your daddy tonight, huh? And I'll see you in the morning."

Mia squirmed, so Lynn set her back down on the floor. "I'm going to get out of your hair. Not to mention Thai is probably ready to tear my house apart out of boredom."

Her kitten. Nathan had nearly forgotten about him. He wondered if he'd ever have the opportunity to see her place and meet the kitten that had Lynn sneaking around her house with a rolling pin. "We definitely don't want him to do that." He checked to make sure Mia was staying out of trouble before walking with her to the front door where she'd left her things.

Lynn picked them up and turned to face him again. The moment she lifted her chin and her pretty hazel eyes to him, he leaned in a little. The need to put his arms around her and kiss her was nearly overwhelming.

His gaze traveled to her lips for a moment before focusing again on her face. She swallowed hard, shifted her weight to her toes, and pressed a soft kiss to his cheek. It was so brief, he might have imagined it if it weren't for the way his skin zinged from the contact.

"Stay well, Nathan. Good night."

With that, she let herself out. Nathan stood in the doorway and watched as she got in her car and pulled away. That's when it dawned on him.

He was falling in love with Lynn Crosby.

8

With the last of Brooke's furniture loaded into the moving truck, Nathan checked on Mia in the play yard in the shade beneath the tree. Brooke kept the play yard at her house for when she watched Mia on Saturdays. It would be the last thing loaded into the U-Haul. Most of her things were taken over to the house she'd share with Chess after the wedding tomorrow except for necessities she needed to live for the last two weeks.

"Where did you say the girls went?"

Chess sat on the moving truck's bumper. "To do girl things, I guess. Anna insisted Brooke needed to get her nails done, have her hair trimmed. Who knows what else. Brooke was looking forward to it all week." He grinned. "I'm real glad this wedding is a small one. Take it from me—when you decide to get married, make sure she likes small weddings, too."

"I'll add that to the questionnaire I give out to all my potential spouses." Nathan joined him on the bumper, glad to sit down for a few minutes. His mind immediately flew to Lynn for the hundredth time in the last couple of days. "Are you telling me that if Brooke wanted a big, fancy wedding, you'd have called it off?" He was only teasing because he knew full well that Brooke had Chess wrapped around her little finger.

Chess laughed loudly, his deep voice snagging Mia's attention. She smiled big in response. "Nah. I'd marry her anyway. But the small wedding is certainly a bonus." He shook his head. "A lot has changed since I was helping you move into your place last year, hasn't it?"

Nathan remembered that well. He was still getting to know his new-found brother. The decision to leave his home in Florida and move to Texas had been a big one, but he hadn't regretted it once. "It sure has." He turned to find Chess giving him a curious look. "What?"

"How are things going with Lynn? You've talked non-stop about her for weeks, and you haven't said a word about her today."

"I didn't realize you were keeping track." When Nathan's comment was met with silence, he sighed. "I care about her, Chess. More than I should. But it's complicated."

"Are you in love with her?"

Nathan stood from his spot on the bumper. "It could easily happen if I let myself. But there's a lot I don't know about her, and I'm not sure why she's reluctant to talk about it. After Mia's mom—"

"—who was nothing like Lynn."

"—I just don't think I could handle watching someone else walk away from Mia."

"Or you." Chess nodded slowly. "I get that. But you deserve the chance to grow old with someone, and Mia deserves to have a mother who cares about her."

They both knew how rare it was to have both parental

figures in their lives, and what it was like to grow up without them, or with an unhealthy family life in general.

Nathan wanted nothing more than for Mia to have a mom she could go to for help. Someone to teach her and reach her in ways that Nathan would never be able to. But how was he supposed to know that Lynn was the one? That any woman was the right one?

"I've got a lot of baggage I'd be bringing into a relationship. I'm not sure how good of an idea that is." Sure, he'd already told her about a lot of it. But there was a difference between listening to someone chat about his life, and being a part of what that past meant.

"It sounds like she's got some baggage of her own, too." Chess said with a knowing voice. "I think we all do. It just matters how much of it we carry around with us compared to that which we've left behind. The baggage you say you'd be bringing? You left most of that back in Florida." Chess gave his younger brother a pointed look. "There's no sense in dredging it out of the past and adding it to what you have to carry now."

He wasn't wrong. "I hope I'm that smart when I'm as old as you are."

Chess shoved Nathan. "Being the brother with both the good looks and the smarts is a responsibility I'll just have to shoulder."

"Right. Dream on, dude." Nathan laughed for several moments before sobering again. "So, you think I should go for it with Lynn?"

"I can't tell you that. But I do know that I'm thankful every day for what Brooke and I have. If you think there's even a chance that you could find that with Lynn, you owe it to yourself to try."

Nathan nodded slowly. "Thanks, Chess." He tried to fight

back a smile. "For the record? You might have been born with the smarts, but the good looks are debatable."

Laughing together, they closed up the truck and got ready to take everything over to Chess's house. Nathan was glad for the distraction because he wasn't sure what to do about Lynn. What if he told her he was interested in her and she ran for the hills?

He wouldn't do anything to jeopardize Chess and Brooke's wedding. Which meant everything needed to stay the same with Lynn through Saturday. After that? Nathan had a feeling he'd be doing a lot of praying between now and then.

THERE WEREN'T many guests attending the wedding. Maybe thirty at most. But Lynn's fear of being recognized by some random stranger was very real. That's when being in charge of an adorable baby was one of the best things that could happen. People saw Lynn with Mia in her arms, and all comments were directed toward the girl.

If someone did address Lynn, they often asked how she knew the family. It was easy to say that she kept Mia during the day while Nathan was working. That seemed to satisfy everyone, allowing Lynn to avoid any further questioning.

She glanced at the clock on the wall of the sanctuary where all the guests were gathered. They had about ten minutes left before the wedding was scheduled to begin.

Armed with a bag full of snacks and toys, Lynn and Mia had been directed to the row of chairs at the very front. Mia might not remember her uncle's wedding, but at least she'd grow up knowing she was there to witness it.

Mia sat in the chair next to Lynn, a busy board book on

her lap. She seemed content to raise and lower flaps for the time being.

There were plenty of people passing by them, but it wasn't until someone stopped and crouched down in front of Mia that Lynn raised her gaze. Nathan smiled back at her.

"How are you two pretty ladies doing?"

He was probably just being polite, but his compliment still made Lynn's cheeks warm. She'd spent hours with Sharon trying to choose the right dress to wear. She'd worried about showing up to the wedding and being too fancy. Or not fancy enough. Thankfully, she seemed to blend right in with the rest of the guests.

Whether he really meant the compliment or not, she didn't know how to respond. So she chose to update him on his daughter.

"Mia's doing well. Aren't you, bug?"

The little girl babbled something Lynn couldn't quite decipher.

Lynn took in Nathan's black suit, white shirt, and tie. The guy sure did clean up well. In fact, it was a struggle not to stare. Especially right now when he kept watching her, a sweet smile on his face, and his piercing blue eyes drawing her in.

She mentally shook herself. "Shouldn't you be with the groom?"

"I'm going back again, but I wanted to make sure you two were okay. If anything comes up, just wave me over. Seriously."

"I'm just hoping and praying I can keep Mia happy and not ruin the wedding."

Nathan chuckled. "I don't think you have to worry about that."

"I sure hope not. But you might be surprised just how

much of a klutz I really am." She hated the way she talked too much when she was nervous. And right now, between being in the front row for a wedding full of people she barely knew and the handsome man before her that kept getting her distracted, she had all kinds of reasons to be nervous.

Please, God, just help us get through this without messing something up.

Her nerves must have shone through because Nathan placed a warm, comforting hand over hers. "I can't tell you how much I appreciate you being here. Mia's fine. I think Chess and Brooke are just about ready. Thirty minutes from now, we'll be taking pictures and then it'll be time for some cake."

Lynn nodded, suddenly feeling very silly for her reaction. If anyone ought to be nervous, it should be Brooke. "I'm sorry. We're good here, you go help Chess. We'll see you in a while."

He squeezed her hand. Before standing, he leaned in closer and whispered, "I meant what I said. You look beautiful today." With that, he was gone.

Lynn's heart thudded against her ribs as his compliment took root and sent warmth to every cell in her body.

Maybe it was a good thing she was sitting in the front row after all—there were fewer people to see her face had turned pink. She looked down at the pale green dress and reminded herself to thank Sharon for the color recommendation.

Mia kept her busy as everyone took their places, including Chess at the front near the pastor with Nathan by his side. Mia pointed to her daddy who waved at her, earning him a bright smile. He offered Lynn one before turning his attention back to Chess.

Minutes later, music began and the guests turned to watch

as Anna came down the aisle of the small church, her arms full of flowers and a happy smile on her face.

As soon as she reached her spot and turned, the music changed again and they watched Brooke slowly make her way down the center aisle, her arm tucked into Joel's. Her white wedding dress was gorgeous, yet simple. There was no long train, yet the beads and lace created the perfect combination.

What Lynn noticed the most, though, was the way Brooke glowed. She all but floated down the aisle, her eyes on no one but Chess ahead. And when Joel transferred her hand to Chess's, it was clear her intended felt the same way.

That right there was what Lynn wanted some day. To walk down the aisle and be worried about no one but the man she was in love with. For him to look at her—wait for her—with such love.

Joel took a seat on the other side of Mia. The little girl handed him the book she was holding before turning and climbing into Lynn's lap. Lynn wrapped her arms around Mia and held her close as the ceremony began.

It was beautiful, short, and perfect. Lynn caught Nathan looking over at her and Mia twice. Most likely to see how his daughter was doing.

When the ceremony was over, everyone stood and clapped. Mia seemed excited to clap with all the adults. Anna went to the front of the church and raised her hand for attention. Once the room quieted, she spoke.

"Thank you so much for coming. We're going to be taking some pictures of the wedding party. We hope that you'll make your way to the dining hall where lunch will be served. I promise we will all join you before long."

Nathan had told Lynn before the ceremony that they wanted to get a family picture or two that included Mia, but then Lynn would probably watch her for a bit while the rest of the photos were taken. Lynn remained behind as the rest of the guests filed out.

"You did so well!" Nathan scooped Mia into his arms and spun her around. "Thanks for being such a good girl for Uncle Chess and Aunt Brooke."

Mia struggled to get down, but Nathan tightened his grip on her. "Not yet, little lady. Come let us take a few pictures, then I'll bring you back to Miss Lynn."

True to his word, it wasn't but ten minutes before he returned. "Thank you again, Lynn. You've been a lifesaver today." He placed a hand on her arm. "You two should go get something to eat so you're not waiting around here. I'll find you as soon as I can."

Lynn nodded. Mia was starting to get fussy, likely due to hunger. But Lynn wished she could stay there in the sanctuary with Nathan.

By the time she fed Mia, ate a little something herself, and then watched the new married couple cut the cake, she'd had just about enough of crowds. Besides, her young charge kept yawning and was beginning to look droopy.

Other than a glimpse or two, they hadn't seen Nathan since they'd left the photo shoot.

Lynn patted Mia's back as the girl laid her head on Lynn's shoulder. "Come on, bug, let's find a place for you to rest."

She considered the nursery, but someone had mentioned that it was being manned so young children could be left there during the ceremony if needed. Instead, Lynn walked through the church and back to the sanctuary. The doors had been closed and lights lowered. Perfect.

She pushed the front of two cushioned chairs together creating a makeshift bed. The moment she laid Mia down, the girl released a gentle sigh and that was it. Earlier, Lynn had noticed a light blanket in the bag so she took that out and covered Mia before standing again and stretching her back.

It was so much quieter here. With the doors closed, she couldn't hear anyone else, and the peace did wonders for a developing headache as well as releasing the tension in her neck. She looked around the room, admiring the pretty flowers and the way they filled the whole area with their gentle scent.

That's when her gaze landed on the small piano in the corner of the room, and it may as well have been calling to her.

Lynn ran a hand over the smooth surface. Goosebumps peppered her arms as her fingers slid over the top, down the slope, and then rested on the keys.

There was a time when this was where she spent most of her free hours. Allowing her fingers to dance across the keys was her life. Would she still know how to play? Or would the chords escape her?

Even as she wondered, she could see them in her mind. Feel them beneath her fingers. She'd lived for playing the piano, and it wasn't something she could forget. Goodness knows she'd tried.

Lynn glanced at Mia who was still sound asleep. As she slid onto the bench seat in front of the piano, she could easily see Mia so she'd know if the girl started to stir. Mia had proven she could sleep through almost anything at Little Lambs, so Lynn knew she was safe.

She took in a deep breath, held it, and tentatively put some pressure on the keys. The moment that chord filled her ears, she was gone. Whisked away to a time when her life was more carefree. A time when music was her only true concern. A time when music could fix everything.

A single tear rolled down her cheek. She brushed it away,

sniffed once, and poured her heart onto the keys. She allowed the music to carry her away from her parents' disappointment and her failed career. Away from the stalker who'd stolen her confidence and replaced it with fear.

And then there was Nathan.

She knew then that she was falling in love with him. But he didn't even know who she was. Would he walk away from her when he found out the truth?

Unwilling to face that right now, she simply played, and felt a tiny bit of her heart heal in the process.

9

Seeing Chess and Brooke happy was the most amazing part of the whole wedding ceremony—barbecue sandwiches and mini burgers included. Nathan hated that he and Lynn took shifts eating and that he'd been unable to spend meaningful time with her. At the same time, it was a huge relief to know that Mia was well taken care of and happy so that he could concentrate on his brother.

Now that the happy couple was busy thanking their guests for coming, he was free to find Lynn and Mia. The trouble was, he hadn't seen them except for a quick glance when the wedding cake was cut. Where had they gone to?

The first place he checked was the church's nursery and then the kitchen. When he didn't find them there, he went back to the sanctuary. The doors had been shut, but even before he opened them, the sound of piano music reached his ears. The narrow window in each door didn't give him much of a view inside.

The stark contrast between his surroundings and the song took Nathan a moment to recognize the tune: "Walking in Memphis." It reminded him of the version by Lonestar.

He quietly slipped into the sanctuary before closing the doors again.

Lynn wasn't singing, but she didn't need to. The way her fingers caressed the keys, expertly playing each note, had the words playing in his mind. He'd never learned to play an instrument, but he knew enough about music to acknowledge the complexity with which Lynn was playing.

Nathan scanned the room and spotted Mia sleeping peacefully across two chairs, and his heart turned over in his chest.

He approached and eased into a chair near Mia. Lynn's chin raised and her eyes widened in surprise when she saw him. He immediately motioned for her to continue.

To her credit, she never faltered. With one more glance at him, her eyelids lowered as music flowed through her.

When the last notes ended, she opened her eyes again and focused on him. Even in the low lights of the sanctuary, there was no missing the blush in her cheeks or the peace in her eyes.

Nathan approached the piano and joined her on the long bench. "That was beautiful, Lynn. I've always loved that song."

She nodded. "Me, too." She ran a hand along the top of the piano. "It was one of the first songs I learned to play."

"You're a natural. When you said you played the piano, I figured you probably plunked around on it from time to time. But this." He shook his head in awe. "You are incredibly talented. You should do something with your music."

He watched as doubt clouded her features. What happened to make her question her talent? He wanted to know. He wanted to know everything about her.

Suddenly, this seemed like the right time. They were alone—well, mostly alone since Mia was sleeping—and the sanctuary was quiet. Now that the wedding was over, who knew when he'd have the chance to really talk to Lynn again?

He shifted on the bench to face her. "Lynn, I've been thinking and praying a lot lately." He swallowed hard. "You've been so kind to Mia. She's completely taken with you, I hope you know that. And she's not the only one."

As his words sank in, Lynn pulled one corner of her bottom lip between her teeth. Nathan wanted to capture her lips with his then and there. He took in a deep breath to steady the gallop of his heart.

Lynn shook her head and released her bottom lip. "There's a lot about me that you don't know, Nathan. Things I need to tell you—but not here. Not right now." The way she cast a furtive glance at the doors made it seem as though she might be ready to escape at any moment.

What all could she possibly have to tell him? Whatever it was, he was certain they could work through it. Together.

Nathan rested a hand on her shoulder and let his thumb lightly brush against her neck. There he could feel each heartbeat as she looked into his eyes. "We'll find a time to talk and soon. I promise." Mia stirred and he knew that their private moment was likely coming to an end. "I care about you, Lynn. It'd be easy for me to fall in love with you. I'm already well on my way. What I need to know is whether you could feel the same way about me."

He held his breath and counted the pulses of her heart beneath his thumb. What if she turned him down? What if she got up and left without saying anything at all?

He watched a mix of emotions cross her eyes. Her lashes fell, creating dark crescents against her pretty cheeks, only to lift again a moment later. When her lips parted, her soft voice had his entire attention.

"I'm scared, Nathan. Because I'm falling in love with you, too."

Nathan released the air he'd kept trapped in his lungs, a smile tugging at the corners of his mouth. His relief colliding with exhilaration had him leaning in to gently cover her lips with his own.

He took his time, gently exploring her lips in a chaste kiss that blew every other kiss he'd ever experienced right out of the water. Lynn's hand went to the back of his neck and he moved to pull her closer when the sanctuary door banged open.

Lynn jumped and their kiss ended way before Nathan wanted it to. He looked toward the entrance to find Chess standing there, an amused look on his face. "Sorry, guys. Brooke and I are about to head out, and we didn't want to leave before saying goodbye." He turned and spoke to someone in the hallway, then held the door open for Brooke to enter the sanctuary before him.

Nathan admired Lynn's beautiful face for a moment before taking her hand and helping her stand. He'd thought about keeping her hand in his, but she stepped away as Mia sat up and rubbed her eyes with one fist.

Brooke and Lynn reached the little girl at the same time. Brooke smoothed some hair out of Mia's eyes. "You did such a great job, Mia. I'm proud of you. And your dress looks so pretty."

As though she'd just remembered her dress, Mia stood from the chair and ran a hand down the fabric to straighten it with her chubby little hands. Both women chuckled.

Chess moved to stand next to Nathan. "You'll have to fill me in later. Although I think I can guess at the outcome of your discussion." His eyes twinkled.

Nathan tipped his head toward the women. "And I think

you have something more important to worry yourself about right now."

Chess grinned. "Yes. Yes, I do. I just wish I could take her on a proper honeymoon now."

Brooke was in the middle of some college classes, and the couple had decided to wait until summer to go somewhere together. They'd have the weekend before life would return to normal. Or, at least, their new normal.

"It's just a couple of months. It'll be worth the wait." Nathan went to lift Mia in his arms. "Come on, sweetheart. Let's go wave to Uncle Chess and Aunt Brooke."

Lynn picked up the diaper bag, but Nathan took it from her and slung it over one shoulder. Then, in a move he knew was probably bold, he reached for her hand. The moment he had it nestled within his, he felt her relax and gave her hand a gentle squeeze.

This. He could so get used to this.

IT'D ONLY BEEN a few days since he'd arrived in Fort Worth, but Jeb was already going stir-crazy. Yesterday, he'd tried to occupy himself by going to a mall and looking around. It didn't work, though.

Before leaving Tennessee, Jeb set up alerts on his social media accounts to inform him if someone posted anything to do with Bethany Truitt. He often got pings for just Bethany, or even Truitt associated with other things.

Every time his phone pinged, he was checking to see if there was another sighting of Bethany. Each time, he'd been disappointed.

He'd convinced his brother he'd only be gone for a few days, but Jeb knew full well he'd wait however long it took.

Even if it meant spending way too much time staring at the drab wallpaper of his hotel room.

He expected much the same this time when his phone sounded with an all-too-familiar ping. This time, he wasn't disappointed in the target content.

"I saw Bethany Truitt go into a church in Dallas earlier. Check it out!" The accompanying photo left no doubt about it.

There was Bethany, a playful smile on her face, just before entering the church. Thankfully, the name of the church was prominently displayed on the glass door she was about to walk through.

Jeb's heart raced as he did a search for the church online. Barely taking time to pull the hotel room door closed behind him, he flew down the stairs and hopped into his car.

If he was going to catch her, he had to get moving. Who knew why she was at the church or how long she'd be there. He couldn't risk missing this opportunity to finally see her again.

LYNN COULDN'T HAVE BEEN MORE surprised than when Nathan took her hand in his in front of his family. There was something about standing out there with everyone, waving goodbye to Chess and Brooke, and feeling as though she belonged with him and Mia. It was an entirely new experience, and one she was certain she could quickly get used to.

The guests thinned out after that. Before long, it was time to head home. Anna volunteered to hold Mia so that Nathan could walk Lynn to her car. Once there, she unlocked the door then turned to face him.

"I think that was successful. Mia did so well, too. She's such a sweetheart."

Nathan smiled, his eyes never leaving Lynn's face. "Yeah, she did. Mostly thanks to you." He leaned forward and pressed a light kiss to her cheek near the corner of her mouth. "I've got plans with Joel and Anna this afternoon and tomorrow. I'm sure you could join us."

Lynn shook her head. "I wish I could, but you should be with your family. Besides, I really do want to have the chance to talk." The thought of telling him everything had her stomach in knots.

"Of course. I'll talk to Anna and Joel and see if they can keep Mia one evening this week so I can take you to dinner or something." He smiled. "What do you say, Lynn Crosby. Will you go out with me?"

"I'd love to."

Lynn enjoyed the feel of Nathan's arms around her as he kissed her gently. It wasn't until they'd finally stepped apart and she climbed into her car that the nerves started building.

Would he continue calling her Lynn after she told him about her past? Or Bethany? Or would he want nothing to do with her at all? At least it'd be a relief to tell him the truth about everything.

"Lord, please help Nathan to understand why I didn't tell him about everything sooner." She thought back to the wedding and smiled. "And thank you for an amazing day."

"THERE YOU ARE."

The moment Jeb caught sight of Bethany, it was as though the last two years without her melted away. She'd been lost.

To him. To the world. And here she was again. He'd found her. And he'd make sure he never lost track of her again.

Apparently, she'd been attending a wedding. He parked in a small lot across from the church where he could still watch without being noticed.

The newlyweds climbed into a car to the cheering and clapping of friends and family. Bethany clapped as well, a big smile on her face.

A smile he'd never once forgotten.

Now that he knew where she was, he was confident that, one day, she'd offer that smile to him.

After the newlyweds' car pulled away from the church and disappeared, the small crowd out front made their way back into the church.

That's when Jeb saw Bethany holding hands with a man standing next to her. He squinted as jealousy coursed through his veins.

Who did that man think he was? Who was the child the man was holding?

Bethany must have forgotten her past. Forgotten about fame and the people like Jeb who'd made it possible.

He'd remind her where she came from. Show her it was a mistake to walk away from it all. And then she'd understand how they belonged together.

10

L   ynn read over her letter to Perry one last time before folding it and slipping it into an envelope. Once it was addressed and stamped, she put it on the table near the door so she'd remember to stick it in the mailbox on the way out.

With any luck, Mom and Dad would give it to her this time.

Satisfied and feeling hopeful, Lynn glanced at the clock. It was Monday morning, and she still had thirty minutes before she needed to leave for work. She'd awakened earlier than normal, excited about the week to come.

Saturday still seemed like a dream. Everything about it was perfect: From how well she and Mia got along to the connection she and Nathan had made.

Even now, thinking about the way it felt to be held in his arms had her knees feeling weak.

She couldn't wait to hear from him about when they could go out to dinner. At the same time, knowing she'd be telling him the truth about her past was a scary thing.

It'd be good to get that out there. She just wished she

knew how he'd react. Sharon assured her all would be well. If only Lynn could be as confident about that.

Lynn's attention focused on the keyboard against one wall of the living room. Remembering what it felt like to play at the church had her retrieving a towel from the kitchen. She gently dusted the neglected instrument before sitting on the small bench in front of it.

At first, she just let her hands rest on the keys. It wasn't long before she was playing something. Instead of the usual pain and regret she expected, memories of playing for Nathan floated to the forefront. It reminded her of why she used to live to make music. Of how it felt to be one with the notes, as though they controlled her fingers all on their own.

The next time she looked up at the clock, she realized she was nearly late. She gave Thai a last pat, grabbed her stuff, and headed out the door.

She didn't want to miss Nathan dropping Mia off. Her lips tingled as she remembered his kisses.

Yes, this was going to be a great week.

―――――

THAT EVENING, Jeb hoped to catch some glimpses of Bethany in the little house she lived in. She didn't seem to open the blinds, though. It was disappointing. Although hearing her play music that morning had been the highlight of his day.

When she left the house, she immediately got in her car. No strolls down the sidewalk or hanging out in the backyard.

It made it nearly impossible for him to find a casual way to bump in to her.

He'd missed her for so long. It was hard to be this close, and yet so far away.

What if she'd missed him that much, too? What if just

knowing that he was there—that he cared—made her as happy as he was right now?

Jeb realized then that he should've figured out a way to let her know he was back in her life. Much more subtly than last time.

He opened the glove compartment and withdrew a large plastic bag full of the guitar picks he'd collected. Before Bethany quit singing, he'd left her a couple of them. Would she remember?

One advantage to her not opening her blinds was that, once she was home that evening, he was free to walk up to her front door. He pressed a single guitar pick to his lips and then set it perfectly on the little welcome mat.

It'd be the first thing she'd see when she left for work the following morning.

LYNN HAD BEEN a little disappointed when Nathan told her yesterday that they'd have to wait until Sunday afternoon for their first official date. At least she got to see him every morning and evening. That would make it easier to wait out the week.

She'd managed to push some of her concerns from her mind as she got ready for work, gave Thai the attention he demanded, and then headed out of the house.

As she crossed the front door threshold, something on the doormat caught her attention. She nearly ignored it and continued on her way except that it looked familiar. She bent down to pick it up and gasped.

The guitar pick with "Bethany Truitt" written on it might as well have been a hot coal. She dropped it again and watched as it clattered to the concrete. With the exception of a guitar pick or two that she kept in her jewelry box as a reminder of the past, she hadn't seen her name written anywhere since she left the music world behind.

Where had this one come from? Someone must have figured out who she was, there was no other explanation.

Her gaze ping-ponged from her car to the houses across the street and back. Nothing seemed out of the ordinary, but the hair still stood up on the back of her neck. She grabbed the pick, shoved it into her pocket, and made sure the front door was locked.

By the time she got to work, her hands were shaking. Sharon noticed immediately and came forward, a baby in one arm. "What happened?"

"Someone knows I'm Bethany."

Sharon's eyes widened. "Someone at Little Lambs?"

"No. Maybe. I'm not sure." Lynn tried to slow her breathing. It felt as though the pick were burning a hole in her pocket. She took it out and showed it to Sharon. "This was on my front porch, and it's not mine."

She suspected Sharon was going to argue against Lynn's suspicions until she saw the pick. "I wonder who left it? No one here has ever acted as though they know something."

Lynn crossed her arms, suddenly chilled. "I should've known I wouldn't be able to keep this up forever."

"Don't go throwing your new life away just yet." Sharon gave her a side hug. "Maybe your landlord's granddaughter recognized you and just wanted you to know. Maybe she's hoping you'll sign the back and leave it there for her."

"I think you're reaching." If only it were something that simple and innocent. All she knew right now was that the pick in her hand was making her feel incredibly exposed. "I'll be right back." She went into the restroom, snapped the pick in half, wrapped it in a paper towel, and put it in the trash.

It didn't matter if some kid wanted an autograph. If that were the case, he or she could come and ask for one.

By the time Lynn got back out to the nursery, she was starting to feel a little less shaky. Especially when she saw Nathan and Mia waiting at the counter. Just having the chance to talk to them both helped a little.

Even though her interaction with Nathan was short, the slight brushing of his hand against hers had her heart singing. She went to work with Mia in her arms. Focusing on her little charges was exactly what she needed.

She'd get through today, see Nathan again tonight, and everything would be fine. It was probably just her landlord's granddaughter, like Sharon said. Lynn would mention it to her landlord tomorrow. That would probably clear everything up, and she'd feel silly for reacting so strongly.

Later that evening, she called her landlord and ended up having to leave a message on the machine. There were no new guitar picks waiting for her at the front door. She'd watched traffic all the way home for signs of someone following her. No strange cars on the street.

Even still, she moved a kitchen chair and put it in front of both the front and back doors. If someone was going to break in, he'd make a whole lot of noise doing it. Thai meowed as he looked up at her in curiosity.

Lynn chuckled. "I know. I was a little crazy before I became the crazy cat lady." She bent down and scooped him into her arms. "Come on, let's go to bed." She turned the kitchen light off, but flipped it back on again before leaving the room.

The next morning, she was relieved to find no more guitar picks on her door mat. By the time she got to work, she wasn't feeling nearly as vulnerable as she was before.

That's exactly why, when she went out to her car to get

her lunch box later that day, she didn't think anything about the piece of paper stuck under her windshield wiper. It wasn't unusual to find advertisements for local restaurants offering lunch specials.

Lynn pulled the paper out and was about to crumple it up when she noticed it was blank except for something taped to the other side. When she turned it over, another guitar pick stared back at her. She dropped the paper and pressed a hand to her mouth.

She'd been kidding herself. It was happening again.

What was she supposed to do? She didn't want to touch the paper again, but if this turned into something more, she might need it as evidence. Lynn carefully retrieved it by one corner, took a picture with her phone, and went back inside the day care center.

She found Sharon in the nursery and held the paper out, her hands shaking.

"He knows where I work. This isn't a coincidence. It's him."

Sharon had been burping an infant who'd fallen asleep on her shoulder. She stood carefully and laid the baby down in one of the cribs.

She took a closer look at the paper. "Call the police."

"And tell them what? That I've been living under a different name and someone is leaving guitar picks? The guy got away and was never arrested in the first place. They won't be able to do a thing." Lynn ran her fingers through her hair several times before letting her arms drop. "He hasn't broken into anything. No scary messages. I can't even give enough evidence to completely convince myself the guy's back because they gave out a million of these stupid guitar picks back in the day."

"You could come stay with me and Walt for a few days."

Lynn shook her head. "I can't do that. I can't just come live with you forever." She groaned. "I hate this. I should have known better than to move back to Texas. If I'd been smart, I would've moved to Nevada. Oh, or Alaska. I could have disappeared there."

"Right into the belly of a grizzly bear." Sharon snagged Lynn's arm and pulled her to one of the rocking chairs. "You need to take a few breaths."

Lynn tried to relax as she sank into the chair.

Sharon dragged another one closer and sat down as well. "So far, we don't know that this is the same guy who was stalking you before."

"True." Sharon was the only person Lynn had told the whole story to. At the time, the stalker had not only broken into her bus to get to her, but had followed her from concert to concert for months before that, yelling that he was in love with her.

Whoever this was, he seemed relatively hands-off. Maybe it would stay that way.

She sighed and shook her head. "You're right."

"So we keep on keeping on. We'll go to Nathan's class Saturday and learn how to beat the snot out of anyone who does mess with you, and hopefully this will all turn into a non-issue." Sharon paused. "You need to tell Nathan. It can't hurt to have a strong guy like him on your side."

That had one corner of Lynn's mouth inching upward. "No, it certainly wouldn't. We're having dinner Sunday afternoon. I'll tell him then." Only she wished they didn't have to meet somewhere in public. The thought that someone might be watching them sent shivers down her spine.

She just had to keep her cool. If it was simply an anonymous fan, Lynn couldn't let him mess with her life. She'd worked too hard to rebuild one to let it slip through her fingers.

AFTER EVERYTHING that happened at the wedding, Nathan found seeing Lynn briefly at the Little Lambs each day wasn't nearly long enough. He'd spoken with his family. Unfortunately, he wouldn't be able to take Lynn on a proper date until Sunday afternoon.

Nathan wanted it to be just the two of them, and Saturday night would've meant inviting her to join them at family dinner. He took some solace in the fact that Lynn seemed just as disappointed in the delay as he was.

So he'd wait. At least he'd see her at class on Saturday, which was something. But by Thursday evening, he decided he didn't want to wait any longer.

That evening he accepted the diaper bag from Lynn. Before leaving with Mia, he cupped Lynn's elbow in his hand. "Will you meet us at the burger place for dinner tonight?" He didn't expect the flash of hesitation in her eyes that triggered a burst of apprehension in himself. "No pressure at all. We were going there to eat and thought you might be in the mood for a burger, too."

Great job, Nathan. Nothing like being too pushy. He'd thought the offer was a good idea. Now he wasn't sure after her unexpected reaction, and he wished he'd kept his mouth shut.

Lynn shook her head. "It's not that at all." There was an almost unnoticeable pause. "I'd love to meet you over there."

They settled on a time, he squeezed her hand, and headed out with Mia.

An hour later, he'd claimed a table for them, and they

only had to wait a few minutes before Lynn walked through the door. She seemed to scan the room for several seconds and headed their way.

She raised a hand in greeting and smiled. "Hey, guys. It's busy in here tonight." She glanced around the room again before sitting down with them.

"We can order to go and eat at the park or something instead. It is a little noisy."

He thought she was going to agree before she finally shook her head. "No, this is fine. Thanks, though."

Lynn told him what she'd like, and he left the girls at the table to place their orders at the counter up front. When he returned with their drinks, Lynn was still looking nervous.

He slid into the seat beside her. "You okay? Did something happen at work today?"

"I'm sorry." She took one of the cups he'd offered. "It's just been one of those days. How about you? Did anything interesting happen with classes?"

She was clearly deflecting. But if she didn't want to talk about it now in a room full of noisy people, he was going to respect that. Nathan told her about one of his new students as they ate their dinner.

The evening went by way too fast and before he knew it, they were walking back out to the parking lot together. He held her hand in his and noticed her grip tighten a little as they crossed the lot to her car. She pulled her keys out and quickly unlocked it.

"Thanks for suggesting this. It was nice to see you for more than a few minutes at a time. It seems like forever since the wedding, doesn't it?"

"Yes, it does." Nathan shifted a squirmy Mia from one hip to the other. His daughter wasn't going to wait much longer to get down and run around. He placed a hand on Lynn's shoulder and leaned in close. When she tipped her chin up a little, he kissed her, enjoying the way her soft, warm lips felt against his own. "I'll see you tomorrow morning, and I'm looking forward to this weekend."

"I am, too." She leaned in for one more brief kiss. "Thanks again for dinner." She reached for Mia's hand. "Bye, bug. Be good for your daddy tonight."

With one more wave, Lynn got into her car and soon disappeared from view.

Nathan felt better after spending a little extra time with Lynn. But he couldn't help but feel there was something going on. He could only hope she'd open up about it on Sunday.

———————

ANGER COURSED through Jeb's veins as he watched Bethany kiss the man she'd been with at the church. How dare she? Especially after knowing that Jeb was back in her life again?

Maybe he'd been too subtle in his attempts to reach her. There's no way Bethany would be with that guy if she really knew he was there.

Jeb needed to do something more obvious, but what?

Several ideas presented themselves, but Jeb didn't want to jump into things. He'd think it through. Formulate a plan.

And find a way to win Bethany's heart.

———————

NATHAN WAS glad to see Lynn come into jiu-jitsu class with her friend, Sharon. While he'd seen Sharon at Little Lambs before, this was the first time they were officially introduced.

Sharon shook his hand. "Lynn spoke highly of your class. I'm excited about it."

Nathan noted the wedding band on her left hand. "Your husband is always welcome to join us as well."

She laughed. "Oh, he'd probably enjoy it. But he was more than happy to take this opportunity to go to the gun range for a while. Maybe I can convince him to come next week."

"I hope he'll give it a try. Though I can't fault him for wanting to go to the range, either." While Nathan didn't do a lot of shooting, Chess did. Nathan found going with him was a great way to spend some quality brother time together.

He turned his attention back to Lynn and found her watching the main door of the building. A handful of moments later, her gaze swiveled to him and a small blush crept into her cheeks.

Nathan stepped closer and lowered his voice. "Is everything okay?"

Lynn nodded once. "Sorry, just distracted this morning."

He wanted to ask her what was going on, but another student walked in, and it was time to get the class started.

He was satisfied to see Lynn relax a little more with Sharon there. The two women partnered up during practice, and the sound of Lynn's frequent laughter had his heart jumping in his chest.

By the end of class, the tension he could see in Lynn seemed to melt away. The physical exertion of the class had her face glowing as she and Sharon talked. He dismissed class, Lynn excused herself and went to the restroom, leaving Nathan to thank Sharon again for coming.

He considered whether he should bring Lynn up at all. "I've noticed Lynn hasn't quite been herself lately. I hope everything is okay."

Sharon hesitated, which only made Nathan's suspicions jump into high gear. "Things have been a little rough the last few days. I think she's going to explain that when she sees you tomorrow." She glanced at the restroom door as though she were hoping Lynn might appear just then.

Nathan took pity on her, not wanting her to feel uncomfortable. "Well, it was great to have you here. I hope I'll see at least you again next weekend."

"I'm planning on it." Sharon smiled again as Lynn approached them.

"Thanks for the class, Nathan."

"Of course. I'll pick you up tomorrow?"

She nodded, a smile on her face, but a flash of something in her eyes that he couldn't quite interpret. "Absolutely. I'll be ready."

Nathan laid a hand on her shoulder and gave it a squeeze. "I'll see you then."

He watched as the two women left the building. He'd been looking forward to the dinner with Lynn tomorrow, and that was still the case. Except now he couldn't stop wondering what it was Lynn wanted to tell him.

11

L ynn glanced at herself in the bathroom mirror for at least the tenth time. The lilac-colored sundress she'd chosen to wear still looked fine. So did her hair. After agonizing over what to do with it, she'd finally pulled part of it back and braided it, leaving plenty to fall down her back and even some tendrils that gently framed her face.

No, it wasn't her appearance that was the problem. She zeroed in on her own eyes looking back at her. There was no missing the nervousness there and the way she was frowning at herself.

She was finally going on a real date with Nathan, the guy she was rapidly falling in love with. This should be an event she anticipated with butterflies in her stomach. Not only because of the significance of their date, but also because she hoped he'd pull her close and kiss her again.

Making sure her lip gloss was fresh and her hair smoothed down should be her main worries tonight.

Instead, all Lynn could think about was how she was going to tell Nathan that her given name wasn't really Lynn.

She groaned and tipped her head back to look at the ceiling.

She'd lost count of how many times she'd replayed the conversation in her head. Last night, she'd even had dreams about it.

Sometimes, the scenario ended with Nathan promising her that none of it mattered, and that he wanted to be with her whether her name was Lynn, Bethany, or something else entirely.

Then there were other times where her blasted imagination had him walking out of the restaurant, after calling her a fraud, without once looking back.

That's when tears would spring to her eyes as dread sat on her chest like a lead weight.

A small meow at her feet tugged at Lynn's attention. Only then did she realize a small tear had escaped and started its trek down her left cheek. She swiped it away and bent to pick up Thai. She cuddled the kitten close.

He started purring immediately, the sound reverberating through her, a distraction that relieved her mind of the worst-case scenarios. "Thanks, boy. I needed this."

Thai was going to get hair on her dress. Then again, that was preferable to the way her face was going to look if she full-on ugly cried. Over something that hadn't even happened yet.

She carried the kitten to the living room and sat on the recliner. Thai quickly curled up on her lap and purred himself to sleep. As she gently rocked them back and forth with the toes of one foot, Lynn let her eyes slide shut.

"Lord, I know I keep trying to control things that I have no way of controlling. You know my heart and my situation. Please give me the right words to say, and please help Nathan to hear me out." She sighed, releasing some of her pent-up nerves along with the breath from her lungs. She continued to stroke Thai's soft fur as they rocked.

Lynn thought about Nathan and what their relationship was currently like. She resisted the urge to ask God to keep them together. "I want Nathan and Mia to continue to be a part of my life." Because as much as it hurt to think about him severing their relationship now, it hurt even worse to think of losing him and Mia entirely. At least, if she still saw them—still spoke to them—there were possibilities for the future. She watched her parents take Perry and disappear from Lynn's life. Seeing that happen with Nathan and Mia was one of her worst fears right now.

A favorite song from church settled on her heart. Despite a one-eyed judgmental look from Thai, Lynn got to her feet. She carried the kitten to her keyboard and settled him on her lap after sitting down. He seemed content with the transition and closed his eyes again.

Lynn allowed her fingers to still as they touched the keys of her keyboard. Then, she began to play "Seek Ye First" as she poured her worries into the song. Her situation didn't change, but it felt lighter somehow.

Maybe the outcome of today was unpredictable. But there was one thing she knew for sure: she cared about Nathan, and he deserved to know the truth.

She respected him too much to not tell him.

If only she'd told him sooner. Although looking back now, she wasn't entirely sure when the perfect time to tell him would have been.

Lynn realized she'd stopped playing the keyboard. She glanced down at Thai. "I guess now is the perfect time."

A knock at the front door had Lynn jumping to her feet, and a less-than-happy Siamese landing on all four of his with an irritated twitch of his tail.

Lynn brushed off the cat hair as she opened the door. And there he stood: The most handsome man she'd ever met. He wore blue jeans and a black t-shirt. The slight breeze outside tousled his blond hair and brought the scent of his aftershave wafting to her nose.

But above all, it was the brilliant smile meant only for her that had her heart rate racing.

"Hey." He stepped closer and placed a kiss to her cheek. "You look beautiful." His eyes twinkled. "It's nice to see you without the additional audience of my students or daughter."

"I know what you mean." Lynn had worried she might not know what to say when he came to pick her up. But the feel of his hand holding hers now had her relaxing a little. She lifted her chin to smile at him.

As though he could read her mind—or maybe he simply needed the contact as badly as she did—Nathan leaned down to kiss her. A slow kiss that had Lynn's legs growing weak as his warmth and attention drove most of her worries away. At least until he broke their kiss and smiled into her eyes.

They were going to be okay. They had to be.

"Shall we?" He held an arm out to her.

Lynn happily took it and allowed him to escort her out of the house.

Once at the restaurant, they settled in with an appetizer and drinks while they waited for their meals. She'd asked him about Mia and his job. He asked if she'd heard anything from her sister, to which she'd sadly had to answer that she hadn't.

Now they were both sitting silently, a heaviness in the air. Lynn popped the last bit of a mozzarella stick in her mouth and returned Nathan's smile.

This was the time. Right now—this lull—was when she was supposed to start telling him about her past.

"Nathan, I—"

"Look, Lynn, if you—"

They both stopped and laughed, the sound breaking some of the tension. Lynn shook her head. "I'm sorry."

"No, don't be. Look, I know you've got something you want to say, but you seem really hesitant. I don't want you to feel uncomfortable. Or pressured in any way."

His words and concerned expression had Lynn's heart melting right along with some of her worries. "I appreciate that. I'm not going to lie about being nervous. But it's something that I need to tell you. I hope and pray you'll be able to understand." She swallowed hard.

Just as she was about to begin, raised voices floated to them from the front of the restaurant.

Nathan leaned a little over the table and lowered his voice. "I wonder if someone tried to skip out on their bill."

Lynn was beginning to wonder, too, until a small group of people skirted past several of the employees and headed in her direction. Her gaze went to a window where she could see people cupping their hands by their eyes as they peered in.

"Oh, no." *Please, God, not right now. They can't have found me. Not before I was able to tell Nathan.* Her stomach rolled as her worst fears were realized.

One of the men at the front of the group had a cell phone out, seemingly recording a video. "Bethany, what have you been up to since you left the music industry?"

JEB WISHED he could see through the restaurant window well enough to witness Bethany's shock. From the moment he'd announced her presence on social media, he'd hoped people would investigate to see if he was right. This turnout? Way beyond his expectations.

And it served her right, too. What was she thinking going out with that guy again? And after everything Jeb had tried to do to show her he was back.

It was time she faced reality.

Bethany needed to return to her roots. Her music.

Return to him.

NATHAN STRUGGLED to understand what was going on. Why did that man refer to Lynn as Bethany? And why wasn't she correcting him? What did any of this have to do with the music industry?

Lynn stood from her seat as her mouth opened and closed again. When she looked at him, Nathan could see that this was way more than anything he'd imagined over the last week or two. He'd thought maybe she had extra debt she was worried about. Or a health concern. He never, in a million years, could have imagined this.

He wanted an explanation. To know exactly what was going on. But more people were pouring into the restaurant. This wasn't the place.

Nathan pulled some money out of his wallet, placed it on the table to pay for their meal, and then put a protective arm around Lynn's shoulders.

There was no ignoring the warning blaring in his head or the way his stomach was twisting into knots. All he knew right now was that they needed to talk, and they certainly couldn't do so here.

Lynn's jaw was clenched so tightly, he could see the tension in her neck.

He pushed their way through the crowd, refusing to say a word, and thankful that Lynn said nothing as well. The last thing they needed to do was encourage this crowd of people.

Thankfully, Nathan had found a parking spot very close to the restaurant. They were able to get into his Jeep and on the road quickly. He kept an eye on his rearview mirror, but never did see anyone that seemed to be following them.

Even still, he took his time winding his way through town until he pulled up in front of Lynn's place.

She still hadn't spoken about what happened, and he didn't ask for an explanation. Not yet. Instead, he walked around to her door and opened it for her. "I think it'd be better to go inside and talk."

Lynn nodded, took the hand he offered, and stepped down. As soon as she had her balance, she let go of his hand.

Nathan tried not to take the fact she didn't continue to hold his hand as a bad sign of their conversation to come.

He followed them inside where she got them both a glass of ice water and they settled on the couch in the living room.

Nathan replayed what happened at the restaurant in his mind. Surely the guy had been mistaken. But why hadn't Lynn corrected him? Had she been lying to him about who she is? If so, what else could she be holding back?

Those old insecurities he thought he'd put behind him shoved their way back to the surface again. Nearly everyone he'd counted on lied to him in a big way: His birth parents, his adoptive parents, and even Mia's mother. He didn't know how to handle it if Lynn had been doing the same.

She deserved the chance to explain. He deserved the chance to hear it, too.

He didn't touch his water, but watched as she took a long drink of hers. Only after she put the glass on the coffee table did she finally turn to him, her eyes swimming with unshed tears.

"I was going to tell you today. You shouldn't have had to find out like that."

"Honestly? I'm still not sure what I've found out. I'm confused, Lynn. Or is that even your name?" So much for giving her time to explain. He hated the hurt in her eyes in response to his words.

But instead of crying or shutting down, she straightened her spine and gripped her hands in her lap. Her knuckles turned white. "Lynn is my sister's middle name, and Crosby is my mom's maiden name." She paused. "My real name is Bethany Truitt." She held up a hand and hurriedly continued. "Please give me a chance to explain."

Nathan motioned for her to do so even though his head was already spinning. So the guy at the restaurant was right. It took effort to keep his face neutral as he listened to how she'd pursued a music career against her parents' wishes.

He had a hard time understanding how her parents would've cut her out of their lives for following her dreams. Had she talked to them about it? Did they really understand how important it was to her? Did she try to involve them in her life after she left the house, or did she just leave home behind without looking back?

She told him about how she'd finally decided to leave the music industry because they kept pressuring her to turn her back on her morals.

Nathan had a lot of respect for that.

But then she made up a name. Disappeared.

Why? If she'd really followed her heart and what she thought was best for her life both when she left home and when she left the music industry, then why not own it?

And why hide it from him?

Unless she didn't trust him as much as she thought he did.

That thought hit him like a blow to the chest. He struggled to refocus on her words.

"I wanted to tell you earlier. I almost did several times. It's just..." Lynn shrugged, her shoulders slumping in defeat. "I guess the timing never did seem right. Which I know is only an excuse. Because there's never a right time to tell someone something like this." She gave a wry chuckle. "As demonstrated today."

"I've got to admit being ambushed at the restaurant by a bunch of old fans and media isn't exactly the best way to find out my girlfriend isn't who I thought she was." He realized he'd used the word *girlfriend* and flinched when the flash of surprise and hope in her eyes was quickly chased away by disappointment.

That was certainly an emotion he was more than familiar with.

A big part of him wanted to reach for Lynn. *Bethany.* And reassure her they could figure this out. At the same time, his thoughts shifted to Mia.

His little girl had already lost more than she ever should have. Maybe he couldn't protect her from everything all her life, but he could protect her while she was young. He had to.

Watching Lynn now—he just couldn't think of her as Bethany, not yet—had his heart aching. He'd pictured having a life together. He could see Lynn tucking Mia in each night, or holding a little boy with her eyes and his smile. But now... Had he let his emotions get in the way of his better judgment?

When things got difficult before, she dropped everything and disappeared, creating a new life for herself. Now that her real identity had been revealed, would she feel pressured to repeat history?

Lynn finally swallowed. "I'm sorry, Nathan. You and Mia

mean a lot to me…" Her voice broke. "I don't want to lose what we have."

"Neither do I. But there's a lot to think about right now." Nathan stood and walked away from her to a window at the front of her house. He glanced out, half expecting to see a group of people waiting to pounce if the door were to open. Thankfully, with the exception of their vehicles and a couple cars parked across the street, there was nothing to worry about.

He raked his fingers through his hair before turning around. He stopped in front of her, and she lifted her chin to look at him from her spot on the couch.

He had a feeling there was still something she hadn't told him. As much as he hated it, he needed to listen to his gut and not let his lack of judgment get the better of him again.

"I think we need to take some time. At least I need some time to process all of this."

Lynn nodded slowly, the look on her face telling him she'd expected his response. "Should I call you? Or…"

"I'll give you a call, okay? Meanwhile," he pointed toward the front door, "make sure to lock the door behind me."

Nathan thought back to the restaurant and the way all the people there had zero regard for Lynn as a person. The instinct to stay close and protect her kicked into full gear. But he had to think of Mia right now, and he had a lot of sorting to do.

As much as he hated to, he had to walk away for now. "You should call Sharon."

Lynn nodded again, her eyes filling with tears. She stood slowly, her arms crossed tight against her chest.

Before Nathan caved into his instinct to pull Lynn close, he strode to the front door. "Goodbye, Lynn."

He waited outside long enough to hear the deadbolt slide into place before taking the steps two at a time and getting back into the safety of his Jeep.

Nathan let his head rest against the seat. "What else was I supposed to do?" His voice sounded odd in the empty space around him. He groaned, turned the key in the ignition, and tried not to think about the fact that he was leaving behind the first woman he'd ever truly fallen in love with.

12

Lynn wasn't sure what startled her: The sound of Sharon's voice or the loud thuds she made as she sat items on the coffee table. She opened one eye from her position on the couch and squinted against the bright light overhead.

Sharon wasted no time in nudging Lynn's legs off the couch, forcing her to sit up or crash to the floor in an undignified manner.

With a moan, Lynn glared at her friend. "Seriously? You couldn't let a girl enjoy her sleep of oblivion?"

"Nope."

As though Thai were in on it, he meowed and deftly jumped onto Lynn's lap where he made himself comfortable with a rumbling purr.

Sharon handed Lynn a spoon. "I've got ice cream, Twizzlers, egg rolls, and pizza bites. Oh, and ice-cold root beer. Pick your poison."

The selections were carefully laid out on the coffee table. "Lorelai Gilmore would be impressed." She jabbed her spoon at the ice cream. "Can't let it melt, can we?"

Sharon smiled as she handed over the carton. "That's the spirit. So how long are you going to just hide out in your house and pretend the rest of the world doesn't exist?"

Lynn ignored her for several bites. The combination of mint and chocolate melted on her tongue. This wasn't going to fix anything, but there was no denying that chocolate never made a bad situation worse, either.

"It's only been three days." She nodded toward her window where the blinds were closed and curtains drawn. "I've seen a number of cars drive past, slowing in front of my house. And you told me that there were people milling around in the parking lot at the day care center. What else am I supposed to do?"

Sharon raised an eyebrow as though Lynn ought to know the answer already.

When Sharon had told Lynn about the extra people looking for her at the daycare center, she agreed to let Lynn take the week of vacation she'd accumulated, hoping that things would die down and Lynn could return to work after that.

Lynn wasn't convinced. If these people had stayed interested enough for two years, another week wasn't going to deter them.

Yes, she'd rather stay in her house, have the local grocery store deliver to her front door, and be glad she had nowhere to be.

Even if it meant constantly holding onto her phone and checking the screen just in case she'd somehow missed a call from Nathan.

Nothing so far.

She shouldn't have been surprised, but not hearing from him and not seeing Mia at the center doubled her pain and loneliness. "Is Mia doing okay?"

"She is." Sharon took a bite out of her licorice whip. "She's missed you, though."

Lynn almost asked about Nathan but stopped herself.

Apparently her thoughts were written on her face, because Sharon patted her shoulder. "Nathan has looked around for you, too. I told him you had taken a week of vacation."

"I appreciate that."

So Nathan knew where she was. He had her number. He was choosing to not contact her. It'd only been three days, but it was difficult to not let that sting. Everyone else had walked away from her—or pushed her away. Why shouldn't he be any different?

"Hey, that ice cream had finally done it's magic. Don't go getting sad on me again." She got a fresh Twizzler and tried to shove it into the pint of ice cream in Lynn's hand. "He just needs some time. You can't blame the guy."

"I know." It didn't make waiting any easier, especially when one of the possible outcomes might mean not ever talking to him again.

———

JEB COULDN'T HAVE BEEN HAPPIER when he'd watched Bethany's guy leave her house Sunday evening, especially when it was clear he was upset. Jeb's plan to disrupt everything and push Bethany out of her comfort zone had worked.

There was one side effect he hadn't counted on, however.

It'd been four days, and she still hadn't left her house. Other than a quick glimpse of her when she answered her front door for groceries or her friend, he hadn't even seen her.

She was free now. Free to be herself. Free of that low-life she was always hanging around.

She was free to realize just how much she loved him.

But she couldn't do that stuck in her house. Bethany had to go back to work eventually, right?

By Thursday, he was getting more than a little impatient. After sleeping in his car outside Bethany's house two nights in a row, he'd finally gone back to his hotel last night. A shower and change of clothes had been mandatory.

He also took the time to write a letter to Bethany. At the bottom, he signed it and taped one of her guitar picks to the paper.

Now he sat in his car across the street, waiting for the right time to leave the letter. The moment presented itself when pizza delivery arrived. Jeb jumped from his car, jogged across the street, and caught the driver before he'd even gotten out of his own car.

"Hey, fella. You mind if I take that in to her?"

The driver gave Jeb a quizzical look. "I'm supposed to deliver it directly to the person who placed the online order."

The kid was young, and Jeb had a feeling a large tip would probably persuade him. He took a twenty out of his wallet. "I'll give you twenty bucks if you let me surprise my girlfriend. I wanted to put an engagement ring on the pizza."

Without hesitation, the driver smiled, took the money, and handed over the pizza. "You got it, buddy. I hope she says yes." With a tip of his hat, he returned to his car.

Jeb glanced toward Bethany's house, thankful for the first time that she kept her blinds and curtains closed.

Once the pizza delivery kid was out of sight, Jeb went back to his car, taped his letter to the inside lid of the pizza box, and closed it again. After getting a baseball cap from the back seat, he placed it on his head, pulling the bill down far enough to hopefully hide his features.

With his stomach in excited knots, he walked to her front door and knocked.

The moment she opened the door, he breathed in the fruity scent of her shampoo and savored being this close to her. Even if she didn't yet know who he was. Yet.

"I was about to call and see what happened. You are fifteen minutes past the time I was told it would be delivered."

It didn't matter what she said, the words still sounded like music to Jeb's ears. He wished he didn't have to wear the hat or he'd be able to see her pretty eyes better. "Sorry about that. Boss said you could have the pizza free."

That brought a smile to her face as she reached for the box. He didn't want her to open it until she'd gone back inside and he escaped to his car. Hopefully she wouldn't bother checking a free pizza.

"Thank you. I should at least get you a tip."

"Nah. It's all covered. Have a great night."

"You, too." She flashed him another smile and went inside.

Jeb jogged across the street again, ditched the hat, and moved the car. The last thing he needed was for her to spot it right after getting his note.

He headed for the hotel again. Sad to leave her behind, but bolstered by finally receiving another one of her beautiful smiles.

THE SMELL of pepperoni and olives floated from the pizza box making Lynn's stomach rumble in anticipation. She'd been eating mostly sandwiches all week and couldn't wait to sink her teeth into some pizza for a change. She placed the box on the coffee table where a plate, napkin, and something to drink were already waiting.

With her favorite show on and paused, she sat down eagerly and lifted the lid of the box.

Her eyes immediately went to the guitar pick with her old name on it, and she dropped the lid again. The sound of blood rushed in her ears as her heart raced. She continued to stare at the box for several moments before opening it again, careful not to touch the piece of paper.

Hunger pains were immediately replaced with nausea as she read the note.

BETHANY,

I've waited years to see you again. Know that other guy wasn't good enough for you. But I'm here. All you have to do is embrace your music again. Embrace who you once were. You'll see how much we belong together. I'm always here for you.

Forever Yours,
Jeb

"This is a nightmare." She shook her head, never taking her eyes off the box as though it might open up again on her own.

Had this Jeb been the reason she was bombarded at the restaurant the weekend before last? Or were hints of her whereabouts what brought him to the area in the first place?

Either way, it was clear he wasn't going anywhere.

Perfect.

She'd call and report this to the police, although she knew what they would say. They'd take the report and regretfully inform her that there was nothing they could do since Jeb hadn't done anything nefarious.

Instead, she dialed Sharon's number. After briefly trying to tell her what happened, Sharon stopped her and said, "We'll be right over. Don't go outside until we get there."

As if anyone had to tell Lynn that.

Thai rubbed against her shins, causing her to jump a foot. She glared down at him. "You'd be much more useful if you were a watch dog."

Twenty minutes later, she ushered Sharon and Walt into the house before shutting and locking the door securely behind them. "Thanks for coming over. You guys didn't have to do that." She was glad they had, though. "Here, I'll show you the pizza."

Sharon and Walt read the note, a combination of shock and disgust on their features. Walt got his cell phone out and handed it to Lynn. "Go ahead and call the police. This needs to be reported."

Lynn nodded and withdrew her own phone. "I know, I just wanted someone else to see this besides me. Especially since the police would probably take it all with them."

She spoke to them on the phone while Walt snapped pictures of the pizza box and note.

When Lynn hung up, her friends waited expectantly. "They said they'd file my complaint, advised me to take pictures, and call if he does anything threatening." Frustrated, she collapsed on the chair again and resisted the urge to give the pizza box a good kick.

Sharon frowned. "At least we have a first name. I really wish you'd come stay with us for a while." She gave Lynn a sympathetic look. "Have you called Nathan?"

"He all but told me not to. Said he needed time to think." Lynn shrugged as if it were no big deal. She didn't convince herself, much less anyone else. "What? I'm not going to call as though I'm desperate. Or use this as a way to guilt him into talking to me."

What she really wanted was for him to check on her, find out about the pizza, and get all indignant and protective on her behalf. Was that really so much to ask?

She'd gone over their conversation in her head again and again. She'd tried to see it all from his perspective and knew that, if roles had been reversed, she would've been hurt, too. She totally got it.

But that didn't make it any easier.

Sharon put a comforting hand on Lynn's shoulder. "He misses you, too. Trust me." When Lynn turned hopeful eyes to her, Sharon continued, "He always looks around for you when he drops Mia off. And when he doesn't see you, even though he knows you're on vacation, he looks disappointed."

Maybe it shouldn't have, but that offered Lynn a little comfort. "How's Mia doing?"

"She's well. She misses you, too. She's not nearly her happy, bubbly self this week."

Lynn felt bad for the little girl. It'd been weird not going to work, but even weirder to not get her Mia hugs. "Not seeing them this week has been like torture."

"Just hang in there, girl. This isn't going to last forever. Meanwhile, since we don't live that far away, you and I are going to carpool to and from work next week. That way you're never alone coming in and out of your place."

Walt agreed. "We can meet up with you over the weekend if you need to get groceries or anything like that."

Lynn relaxed a little and smiled at her friends. "You guys are awesome. Thank you."

Knowing she wouldn't get ambushed on the way in or out was helpful. But if Jeb hung on this long, another week probably wasn't going to dissuade him. And Sharon couldn't take Lynn to work forever. "I wonder how much a couple of cameras at the front and back doors would cost? You know, the kind that records movement and things like that."

Walt pulled his phone out. "Let's take a look."

13

A hand on his shoulder brought Nathan back to the present and Saturday dinner at Chess's house. Only then did he realize he'd been staring at Mia and Anna playing with blocks on the floor. He turned his head to find Chess watching him with a concerned look on his face.

"I'm fine." Nathan hoisted himself from the overstuffed recliner. "Just tired. Mia has developed an aversion to sleep the last couple of nights."

"A phase."

"Hopefully a very short-lived one." Nathan yawned. Of course, he was having difficulty sleeping himself since his date with Lynn almost a week ago. If Mia hadn't had him hopping last night, there was no guarantee he'd have been sleeping instead.

It'd crossed his mind that Mia might have been having trouble sleeping because she'd missed seeing Lynn at Little Lambs every day last week.

Or maybe that was just him.

He suppressed a sigh.

"Have you talked to Lynn at all?" Chess, always the

blunt one.

Nathan had to admit he often admired that about him. "Nah. Sharon at Little Lambs said Lynn was on vacation this week. I figured maybe she needed the space." As he said the words, he knew that he wasn't being truthful and cringed. It was him who needed the space. He figured a few days would be good to think about their situation. Maybe gain some clarity.

Except the proverbial waters hadn't cleared up one iota all week.

One glance at Chess revealed his older brother knew better.

Brooke walked over and wrapped her arms around her new husband's waist. "For the record, she's probably drowning in all that space you're giving her. Trust me."

Chess pressed a kiss to her forehead and pulled her closer. "There's such a thing as letting too much time pass. It's going to make it harder on Lynn, you, and Mia." He tilted his head toward Anna and the little girl.

"I was hoping I'd have some things figured out this week. You know? Come to some conclusions and feel at peace with them."

"How's that working out for you?" Chess raised an eyebrow.

"Point taken."

Joel announced his presence when he cleared his throat. "Sometimes, it's impossible to reach a conclusion if you've still got unanswered questions."

"I know you're right. You're all right." He had a lot of questions. The problem? Lynn was the only one who would have the answers. It didn't matter how long he waited or how much space he gave her. But seeing her again, being near her, wasn't going to be easy, either.

He'd had many conversations with Chess about the ways Nathan's adopted parents lied to him all the way through his childhood. Mia's mother only increased his distrust. To discover Lynn had been lying to him all along, too, was hard to swallow.

Mia started fussing at Anna, shaking her head when Anna introduced a new game. Nathan moved to retrieve his daughter but stopped when Chess walked up to him.

As though he'd been listening to Nathan's thoughts, Chess said, "Promise me you'll talk to Lynn and get things straight before you lump her in with the others."

Nathan nodded once, his thoughts spinning. He hadn't considered that before, but Chess wasn't wrong. As soon as Nathan heard Lynn hadn't told him everything about her past, he'd assumed she was just like everyone else who had lied to him.

He was still convinced there was something Lynn wasn't telling him. But he hadn't given her a real chance to, either. Or at least given her some reason to believe he'd be able to move past it all.

He sighed as he reached for Mia and tried to console his daughter. After being up half the night, she was no doubt ready for a nap.

Everyone else seemed to sense he needed some time to think. He moved to the room Chess used for a home office and walked back and forth as he rubbed Mia's back. His daughter slowly relaxed against his chest until her even breathing announced she'd finally fallen asleep.

Only then did Nathan open himself up to the possibility that there was more to all of this than just Lynn lying. Was she as miserable as he was right now?

As Mia slept in his arms, Nathan prayed for himself and Mia. And then he prayed for Lynn.

LYNN GLANCED AT THE CLOCK. Nathan and Mia would be at Chess and Brooke's house for the family dinner right about now. Was it silly to feel lonely and a little left out?

She gently stroked Thai's fur as she pretended to focus on the show on television. It was a good thing she'd seen it more than once before, otherwise she'd have no prayer of remembering what this episode was about.

After the whole pizza box incident, Lynn was happy to stay at home. Walt had installed a couple of cameras so she could keep an eye on the front and back doors. Even so, she was starting to feel a little closed in. It was one thing to choose to become a recluse, it was entirely another to be forced into her new role as shut-in.

Thai was practically snoring on her lap. Even though her own foot was falling asleep, Lynn refused to move and wake him. If only she could sleep so peacefully.

She had just returned her attention to the television when her cell phone rang. Unsure of the number, she went ahead and answered it. "Hello?"

"Bethany?"

Lynn blinked at the sound of her mother's voice. She couldn't remember the last time they'd spoken on the phone. "Mom? Is everything okay?"

"We're on our way to the hospital. Your sister collapsed and they think it's her heart." Mom's voice shook. "I felt you should know."

Lynn's surprise stole her voice for several moments. "I'm glad you told me. What hospital are you going to?" She shifted her weight and reached for a nearby notepad and pencil, receiving a nasty look from Thai for her efforts. She wrote down the information. "Okay. Yeah, I've got it."

"And Bethany? Don't come to the hospital. Not yet. Your father wouldn't be happy. I'll keep you updated."

Lynn wanted to argue with her. "Yeah. Call anytime—day or night. Seriously."

"I need to go. Pray hard."

"I will."

The connection went silent, and Lynn set her phone down. A big part of her wanted to ignore her mom's request to stay home and get in the car right now. But what if the stalker was outside? Would she lead him to the hospital and make things worse? What if the press caught wind of where she was going and crowded the hospital?

Either scenario had her stomach aching.

Mom was right. She needed to wait and get an update first. Find out how things were going before she went charging in. Hopefully Perry would get to the hospital, they'd make a change to her medication, and she'd be going home again before the day was out.

"Father, guide the hands and minds of the doctors as they care for Perry." She paused as she thought about the fact that her mom had even called her. That in itself was a huge thing. "Thanks for encouraging Mom to reach out to me and let me know. Please continue to work in their hearts. I miss my family."

For only the hundredth time that hour, Nathan came to mind. There was such a huge contrast between where they were in their lives. Here she was, sitting alone, while he was with an extended family today. It took everything she had not to send him a text and let him know she was thinking about him.

NATHAN CONSIDERED CALLING Lynn all weekend, but every time he got close, he realized he didn't know what to say and then talked himself out of it. He finally convinced himself that waiting until Monday would be the best thing. He'd take Mia by Little Lambs, see Lynn in person, and see if she'd be up to meeting after work.

At this point, talking in person was going to be better than trying to talk on the phone or through texts.

As he got himself and his daughter ready for the day, he kept going over the conversation in his head. He thought he was prepared until he entered Little Lambs and didn't see Lynn anywhere.

Sharon spotted him, waved, and came his way. "Hi, Nathan." She took the diaper bag from him. "Good morning, Miss Mia."

Nathan kept scanning the room, hoping Lynn would walk in from somewhere. "Good morning. I hope you had a nice weekend."

Sharon shrugged. "It was okay. I kind of needed another to recover from it." She reached for Mia.

He gave his daughter a hug and a kiss before handing her over then cleared his throat. "Didn't Lynn come in today?"

Sharon hesitated. "She left me a message early. I guess her sister is in the hospital with some heart trouble. They made the decision this morning to operate. I'm not sure of the details, but Lynn was going over there to wait for more news."

"Did she say which one?"

With a knowing smile, Sharon nodded and told him. "I know she's nervous. I don't think her dad invited her, but she's going anyway." With a pointed look, she added, "Lynn could probably use some support right now. Trust me, she's had a really rough week."

There was no stopping the immediate pang of guilt at only contributing to Lynn's plight. He certainly knew how she felt. "I appreciate the information." He ran a hand over his daughter's silky hair. "Be good for Miss Sharon today, baby. Love you."

Once he got out to the Jeep, he called and spoke to Gregor on the phone. After some schedule reworking, he managed to call in enough favors to get the day off.

Would Lynn be glad to see him if he showed up at the hospital? Or, since they hadn't spoken in a while, would she be upset? He couldn't know until he tried, but he wished he'd reached out to her before now like his gut had told him to do.

Less than an hour later, he arrived at the hospital and headed for the cardiac wing. Once he got there, he looked for someone to ask about Perry. It didn't come to that, though. He spotted Lynn sitting in a chair, one elbow on the arm rest, and her chin in her hand. She sat across from a couple he could only assume to be her parents.

The man had a magazine he was looking at, and the woman next to him worried her thumb.

No one was talking to each other.

The moment he started to approach them, all three pairs of eyes swiveled to him anxiously. The couple both looked disappointed, probably hoping he was the doctor.

But Lynn's beautiful eyes widened with surprise as she got to her feet. "Nathan. What are you doing here?"

"I hope you don't mind. I took Mia by Little Lambs today. Sharon told me why you weren't in, and I wanted to come by and check on you all." He glanced at her parents. Her mother was watching them curiously while her father seemed uninterested after going back to his magazine. "How's your sister?"

Lynn shrugged. "They took her in for surgery about an

hour ago, and we're still waiting to hear something." She ran a hand over her face. "It's been a long night." She studied him with an open expression. "It was nice of you to come by."

Relief flooded Nathan's system. They still had a lot to figure out, but at least she wasn't angry or dismissive. He could deal with that. "I'd like to sit with you all for a while if you don't mind. Mia's with Sharon, and Gregor is covering my classes." He silently prayed that she'd say yes. She looked so tired and worn out. There was probably little he could do to help, but he didn't want to have to walk away and leave her now.

She looked surprised. "That would be nice. Thank you." She turned to her parents. "Mom, Dad. I'd like to introduce you to Nathan Kirkpatrick. Nathan, these are my parents, Ralph and Emily Truitt."

Nathan barely earned a passing nod from Mr. Truitt, but Mrs. Truitt smiled warmly. "It's nice to meet you, Nathan." She looked to Lynn as though hoping for further explanation. "It's good of you to stop by."

"Could I get any of you something to drink from the cafeteria? I'd be happy to make a run down there."

Mrs. Truitt looked to her husband, who didn't bother taking his eyes off his magazine, and finally shook her head.

Nathan turned his focus on Lynn. "How about you? I could get you some coffee. Or a bottle of juice." He noticed Lynn didn't even have water at the moment.

She hesitated before nodding. "I'm actually starving. A bottle of orange juice would be great."

"I'll be back as soon as I can." He resisted the urge to reach for her hand and give it a squeeze before he left.

14

W hat was worse than sitting in a hospital waiting room? Sitting with your father who completely ignores your existence. Lynn sighed. She got the sense that her mother might have been willing to talk or visit a little, but she was hesitant to do so while he was there.

Waiting for news about Perry would have been bad enough. Sitting there with her parents just staring made it seem even longer.

She couldn't have been more surprised to look up and find Nathan approaching them. She'd imagined all kinds of scenarios over the last week or so, wondering what it would be like to see him again. Wondering what he might say, or how she might respond. Sometimes she was upset at him for not bothering to call. Other times, she all but ran into his arms.

But none of that really prepared her for the flood of emotions she actually experienced. Surprise was chased by annoyance that he hadn't called or reached out for so long. But all of that was replaced by relief.

Lynn was so worried about Perry, yet unable to truly

express that with her parents. Having someone there for her was huge.

There was a lot they still needed to talk about, and maybe Nathan was going to tell her their relationship wouldn't work. For now, though, he was here. Right where she needed him to be.

He returned a short time later with a bottle of orange juice and a blueberry muffin. He handed them to her and sat in the chair beside hers.

"Thank you so much." She twisted the lid off the bottle and took a long drink, only then aware of how dry her throat had been. The smell of the muffin had her opening the plastic container it was in and pinching a piece off the fluffy top before placing it on her tongue. Her eyes slid closed in approval. This was exactly what she needed.

When she opened her eyes again, she found Nathan watching her, a look of satisfaction on his face. Her cheeks warmed. A quick check told her that her parents weren't even paying attention. She tried to tell herself that was a good thing. Except that if her long lost daughter introduced her to a man, she'd want to know all about him.

Yet another example of the lack of interest her parents had in her. Lynn swallowed her disappointment right along with the muffin.

Nathan cleared his throat. "Sharon said you took some time off last week. I hope you were able to relax and maybe get some reading in or something."

Was he fishing for why she took the time off work? Even if they were to the point where they were openly talking about everything that happened, this wouldn't be the place to do it. Not within earshot of her parents. Maybe it was pride, but if they didn't have any interest in her life, she certainly wasn't going to give them information for free.

"Let's just say that, by the end of the week, I was going stir crazy." She offered him a smile and hoped that would be enough for now. "How about you? How was your week?"

"It was a long one." He gave her a pointed look. "Maybe we can talk later?" There was no missing the look of hope on his face.

When she smiled her agreement, he rested his arm beside hers, the warmth of his skin sending tingles through her own.

She continued to eat her muffin as they all sat with only the waiting room television to fill in the silence.

It was nearly an hour later before the doctor finally entered through the double doors at one end of the room. Lynn got to her feet along with the others.

Dr. Lang smiled reassuringly. "The procedure went smoothly. Perry is in recovery, but she's still asleep. I'll need to keep her here at the hospital for several days, but I see no reason why she won't make a full recovery."

Mom burst into tears as she turned to hug Dad. Lynn smiled, tears of relief flooding her eyes as well. "Thank you, doctor."

"Of course. A nurse will come let you know when Perry wakes up. At that point, you'll be able to come sit with her. Do you have any questions for me?"

Mom asked several about how to care for Perry once they got her home. The doctor assured her that he'd have full instructions for them before Perry was released from the hospital.

Moments later, he disappeared again.

The waiting room seemed brighter and less ominous than it had been before the doctor came in. Lynn slowly let a lungful of air out as she bounced on the balls of her feet. "Praise God!" She smiled. "I can't wait to see her! She's going to be so surprised I'm here."

That earned her a sharp look from her father. "You know Perry will be okay now. You should leave."

A blow to the stomach couldn't have hit Lynn any harder than his words. She blinked at him, sure she had to have misunderstood him. "But I want to see her. Let her know I'm here and praying for her."

Her father gave a decisive shake of his head. "No one asked you to come here. Your mother and I are here for Perry, just like always, so it's time for you to leave." With that, he opened his magazine again as though he'd given her the time or informed her of the weather.

Lynn's stomach rolled as she turned her attention to her mother. She was the one who let Lynn know about the surgery in the first place. Surely she would say something about Lynn staying.

Mom looked sad, but only said, "Go. I'll send you an update by text later today."

Lynn bit her lip to keep the tears at bay. She refused to cry in front of her parents. Keeping control of her emotions took all she had, and she was afraid if she looked at Nathan, that would be the end. She slung her bag over one shoulder and rushed from the room.

NATHAN FULLY EXPECTED Mrs. Truitt to run after her daughter, but she remained seated next to her husband, sad eyes on the floor at her feet. Nathan may not know enough about the Truitts—or even the history that led to the clear emotional separation between parents and daughter—but he couldn't imagine speaking to Mia like that.

When he didn't leave immediately, Mr. Truitt finally

raised his gaze, his expression stern. Nathan was being dismissed.

He shook his head, amazed at how cold Lynn's parents were being. He intentionally used the name that Mr. Truitt had called Lynn. "Bethany is one of the kindest, most amazing women I've ever met. I hope you know what you're doing by pushing her away."

With that, he left the waiting room. He found her down the hall by the elevators. She was staring out a small window, her back to him, and he heard her sniff as he approached.

"Lynn? Are you okay?"

"I'm sorry." She sniffed again and swiped at her face. "I should be used to this. I should've known better." Her shoulders slumped in defeat. "Knowing my father, he won't even tell Perry that I was here."

"You have nothing to apologize for. Certainly not for anything that happened today." Nathan desperately wanted to step forward and wrap his arm around her, but didn't know if she would welcome it. Or if he even should. Instead, he stood shoulder to shoulder with her and allowed his arm to brush hers. "What your dad said was completely unacceptable. And I got the feeling your mom didn't agree with him."

"Maybe not, but she never speaks against him for any reason. That she even called and told me about Perry's surgery was a shock." Lynn swallowed hard and turned her head to look at him. "How pathetic is it that, after all these years and after my dad acts like this, I still miss my family?"

"It's not pathetic. It's normal." Nathan slipped an arm around her shoulders then. When she leaned into him, he rubbed her upper arm with his thumb. "I've told you some about my childhood. My biological parents were neglectful at best. My adoptive parents deceitful and vindictive. Despite all that, I still sometimes miss them. Or at least miss the idea of a normal family, even if I've never really experienced it."

Lynn leaned her head against his shoulder and nodded. "Maybe that's it. Maybe I miss the idea of a normal family. You know, one that sits in the waiting room together and then bursts into Perry's room with flowers and balloons and takes turns keeping her company until she's released." She quieted for several heartbeats. "I've never experienced a normal family, either. Do you think such a thing even exists?"

Nathan chuckled. "Probably not. Every family has their problems. That's why it's a good thing that, in the absence of biological family, we can choose our own." He was referring more to the way Chess had formed a family, and how they'd all welcomed him and Mia into it. Or how Lynn and Sharon were so close and could support each other.

But as the words left his mouth, he couldn't stop thinking about himself and Lynn. Despite the questions he needed to have answered first, it was way too easy to picture creating a family with her. Too easy to see Lynn rocking Mia to sleep every night. And Nathan waking up next to Lynn every morning? Yep, that was super easy to imagine, too.

He allowed himself to rest his cheek against her head, but resisted the urge to press a kiss to her hair.

That was one thing about Lynn. Once he'd held her in his arms and tasted her lips, it made not doing so all the more difficult.

The woman was addicting. After not seeing her for over a week, he was well aware of what life was like without her, and he didn't like it. But he needed her to be honest with him before he could move forward in their relationship.

"Do you want my opinion about your sister?"

Lynn leaned back a bit so she could see his face. "Sure."

"The hospital is a public place. And your sister, while

under your parents' care, is an adult. I say you go back to the waiting room, get the doctor to see if Perry wants to see you, and if she says yes, your parents will likely have no other choice." When she didn't speak right away, Nathan cleared his throat. "I hope I didn't overstep my bounds. But that's what I would do."

"No, it's a good idea. You're right, my dad can't make me leave here if I don't want to." She straightened and stepped away from Nathan. "Thank you."

"You're welcome." He missed the feel of her leaning into his side. He supposed he should take his leave and give her some space, except it was the last thing he wanted to do.

Lynn surprised him when she asked, "So I suppose you probably have to get back to work, huh?"

"My schedule is clear for the day. And Mia is at Little Lambs until five. I could stick around for a while, if you want me to." *Please, Lynn.* He wanted to help her, even if it meant just keeping her company while she waited to see her sister. And if he was honest with himself, he didn't like the idea of Lynn's parents being unkind to her.

"If you don't mind, that would be great. Thank you."

"Any time. Come on, let's get back in there so you don't miss an update."

She flashed him a brilliant smile that left him with no doubts that staying with her today was the right thing.

JEB SLEPT in his car Sunday night in anticipation of seeing Bethany Monday morning. She'd taken the whole previous week off from work. Surely she couldn't keep that up much longer. He'd been confident she was returning to her normal schedule.

It was a good thing he had been sleeping in his car across the street from her house or he wouldn't have seen her leave in the very early hours of Monday morning.

Equally surprised and curious, he followed her through town to the hospital.

Concerned she might be there for herself, he'd kept his distance and was relieved to find she'd gone to the hospital for someone else. He overheard something about her sister. The couple that appeared to be her parents seemed less than thrilled to see her.

Since the cardiac wing's waiting room was small and virtually empty, Jeb headed back downstairs to wait. She'd have to pass by him to get to her car.

When that guy she'd been seeing arrived at the hospital, to say Jeb was unhappy was very much an understatement. The guy hadn't so much as been to the house since Jeb had Bethany exposed, so hopefully she'd kicked him to the curb where he belonged.

Any hope of that evaporated when the guy went back up to the cardiac wing with an orange juice and blueberry muffin.

Didn't Bethany see how the guy didn't care about her? Why couldn't she understand that Jeb was there, no matter what? He loved her when she was at the top of the pop charts, and he loved her now, too.

He'd make her see that. But first, he had to get the idiot guy out of the picture.

One thing about waiting at a hospital—it gives a person plenty of time to come up with a plan.

15

From the moment Lynn got back to the cardiac waiting room, her father ignored her. How someone could pretend another person wasn't there so completely was beyond her. But her mother, even though she didn't speak, gave Lynn an encouraging smile.

Above it all, though, was the reassurance she had with Nathan sitting to her right. He kept her busy with his tales of Mia. Lynn laughed so hard her stomach hurt when he told her about how Mia had filled the toilet with some of her dolls and then tried to flush them down.

Nathan turned and gave her a stern look. "You wouldn't think it was so funny if you had to pull them out one-by-one and then hope you got them all."

He was right, but that didn't stop Lynn from laughing even harder. "I'm sorry. I hope she never does it again."

"Me, too. The good news is I did snap a picture of her standing beside it, her dolls visible in the toilet, with a content look on her face. It'll serve nicely as blackmail fodder when she gets older."

Lynn glanced at her mother who was smiling at the story.

One from her childhood came to mind, and she considered not telling it, but decided it was from her life and she should be able to do so whether her father approved or not.

"I remember one day, Perry and I were so bored. It'd been raining for what felt like forever, and we were sure we'd done everything we could to entertain ourselves. I finally settled on reading a book, but Perry had other ideas. She came through the room we shared and disappeared into the closet."

Lynn chuckled at the memory. "Curious—and still pretty bored—I opened the closet to find Perry had gotten our mom's make-up bag and was liberally applying everything to her face. In the semi-dark. Oh, she was a mess."

Nathan laughed heartily. "I can't say I'm looking forward to Mia wanting to wear make-up. So what did you do when you saw Perry?"

"We were already bored. The last thing I wanted was be grounded from the few activities we did have available. In desperation, I started wiping the make-up off her face with one of my sweaters."

To Lynn's surprise, her mother chimed in. "And that's when I found them. I never could get the make-up out of that shirt. And you girls still got into trouble."

Dad gave his wife a sharp look, but Mom didn't seem to notice.

Nathan grinned. "What was your punishment?"

"We had to clean the kitchen from top to bottom and make it shine." Lynn shrugged. "At least we weren't bored anymore."

Everyone but Dad laughed.

Nathan started telling another story when a nurse walked into the waiting room, effectively creating a blanket of silence.

"Are you the family of Perry Truitt?"

Dad stepped forward, put an arm around Mom, and said, "We are."

Lynn went to stand near them and nodded her head. A moment later, she felt Nathan just behind her. He gave her hand a gentle squeeze before letting go again.

"She's awake, but still very groggy. Family can visit for a while, but the rooms are small. So a short visit might be best until we get her moved from recovery to a regular room."

Dad barely allowed her time to finish before speaking again. "Her mother and I will sit with her." Then he moved forward as though that settled everything.

Lynn wasn't about to let him take over like that. "I'm Perry's sister. I'd like to come see her for a little while as well."

The nurse smiled. "Of course." She turned to Nathan. "I'm sure we can squeeze four in if your husband would like to come along."

Lynn's cheeks immediately heated as she turned and gave Nathan an apologetic look.

To his credit, he simply raised a hand and said, "I'm just a friend of the family. You three go ahead, and I'll make a run to the cafeteria. Can I get anyone anything?"

Dad ignored him completely, Mom shook her head with a polite, "No, thank you."

Nathan touched Lynn's arm. "Want me to grab you a sandwich or something?"

"That would be great. Thank you."

He smiled into her eyes. "You're welcome. I'll be praying for Perry."

With a final glance his way, Lynn followed the nurse through the double doors, down a hallway, and into recovery room nine where the sound of beeping monitors greeted them.

Dad and Mom rushed forward, and Lynn hung back a little. Perry looked so small in the large hospital bed, and so pale next to the white sheets. She lifted her eyelids and looked at their parents with a small smile on her face. Clearly the poor girl was having a difficult time staying awake.

Lynn remained patient as Mom doted on Perry and Dad looked as though he felt helpless.

Suddenly, Lynn's stomach pitched and her breath caught in her throat. It'd been years since she last spoke to Perry. Waving at her in the window was one thing, but this… What if Lynn walked up there and Perry didn't want to have anything to do with her? What if she upset Perry?

Lynn considered escaping before she was spotted, but knew that wasn't the answer. She'd been waiting for years to see her little sister again. She wasn't about to miss the opportunity.

Instead, she went around to the other side of the bed and approached. When Perry's gaze shifted, Lynn gave her a little wave and a smile. "Hi Perry."

Lynn had imagined their reunion many times, but none of those compared with the way Perry's eyes lit up, her mouth opened wide, and she clasped her hands in front of her.

"It's Bethany! Mom. Dad. Do you see? It's Bethany!"

That's when Lynn went forward and gave her sister a gentle hug and placed a kiss to her brow. "Yes, it's me. I'm so sorry you're going through this. Are you hurting?" When she stood again, Lynn was happy that Perry still held her hand tightly.

Perry nodded. "I'm sore. But mostly, I'm tired." Her eyes closed for several moments before she forced them open again. "Will you come see me again later, too?" She looked right at Lynn.

"Of course I will." She smoothed some of Perry's hair

away from her eyes. "But for now, you need to get some rest."

Perry nodded. She looked around the room at her family and smiled as she allowed her eyelids to fall.

Relief and love flooded Lynn's system in equal measure. Not only was Perry happy to see her, but she wanted Lynn to come back again. It was everything Lynn had hoped for. And much of it was thanks to Nathan not letting her give up and walk away when her Dad wanted her to leave.

She'd wait in the room to make sure Perry was going to stay asleep and then go find him again. She couldn't wait to tell him how well things went.

THERE WERE QUITE a few people in the cafeteria when Nathan arrived, but the hospital had it running like a well-oiled machine. It wasn't long before he'd been able to pay for two ham and cheese sandwiches and bottles of soda.

He didn't want to be gone long in case Lynn needed him. He was proud of her for going back and facing her dad. As a father himself, he was all for respecting and obeying your parents. But from what he'd seen, he wasn't sure Lynn's dad had done anything to earn her respect. Certainly not as an adult, anyway.

With his bag of food, he left the cafeteria and made his way down the hall to the elevator. As he waited, he barely noticed another man walk up and wait as well. Once the doors opened, they both stepped inside. Nathan pushed the button for the eighth floor. The other man chose the sixth.

Only the two of them were in the elevator as it approached the sixth floor. Suddenly, the other guy turned to look at Nathan, an intense expression in his eyes. "You think you know Bethany, but you don't. She hasn't come close to telling you everything about her past—or about me. Stay away from her. I'll find out where you live."

"Are you threatening my family?" Who was this guy? Nathan wanted to push him against the side of the elevator and demand some answers when the doors opened again.

Multiple people walked onto the elevator as the man who'd threatened him pushed through and exited. With one foot on the tracks so the door couldn't closed, Nathan stepped out and looked around, but found no sign of the man.

Knowing Lynn was waiting for him, and not wanting her to run into this guy, he got back on the elevator again. He half expected to see the guy standing there when the elevator doors separated again. Just down the hall, he walked into the waiting room at the same time as Lynn did on the other side.

Nathan waved a hand in greeting, relieved to see that the guy from downstairs wasn't here. "That was a fast visit. Is your sister okay?"

Lynn's smile brightened up the room. "She's going to be okay. She fell asleep again, but she was really happy to see me."

He followed her to some chairs and joined her after she collapsed into one, clearly exhausted. "I'm glad to hear that. I know you were nervous about it."

"We were always so close, but it's been years. I was afraid she might take one look at me and not want anything to do with me." Lynn frowned, but a moment later, her smile broke through again. "She seemed really excited. I want to make sure I come see her after I get off work while she's here. Spend a couple of hours with her." She paused. "I was going to say if my parents let me, but I guess they don't necessarily have a choice. Right?"

"That's right." Nathan smiled at her and handed over the

bottle of soda he'd chosen. "So you are planning on going back to work tomorrow? Mia and I didn't scare you away for good?" He was joking—partially.

Her expression clouded which had Nathan second guessing things again. Was her choice to stay home all week because she didn't want to see him? "It was supposed to be a joke," he said lamely.

Lynn's eyes opened wide. "Oh, I'm sorry. No, it's not you. Things are…complicated." She glanced at the door as though half expecting someone to come through. It looked as though she were going to say something again but seemed to think better of it.

Nathan suppressed a sigh of frustration.

She was still keeping something from him. All he really wanted was for her to open up and tell him what was going on. Especially if it had anything to do with the man downstairs.

Then again, he wasn't even sure where they stood. Which meant Lynn wasn't, either. Especially when he was the one who told her he needed space.

What they really needed to do was talk.

He'd just taken a bite out of his sandwich when Lynn's parents re-entered the waiting room. When Lynn stood, Mrs. Truitt held up a hand to reassure her.

"Perry's sleeping, and the nurse suggested we go get something to eat." She hesitated.

"I'll stay here while you guys go, just in case something comes up," Lynn assured them.

Mrs. Truitt smiled her thanks as she followed her still-silent husband to the hall.

Lynn sat down again and stared at her sandwich. "I wonder if my dad will ever speak to me again." She shrugged. "Is it sad that the only real reason why I care is because I want to be in touch with Perry again? Dad hasn't been my dad for so long, it's hard to really imagine things being any different now." She cringed. "That sounds terrible, doesn't it?"

"To a lot of people, maybe. But it's being realistic." He felt for her. How many times had he faced reality when it came to the people in his life that should've been there no matter what? "Sometimes, real life hurts."

"It sure does."

Nathan worked on his sandwich, though he barely tasted it. He'd hoped Lynn would volunteer to tell him what else was going on in her life. He'd give her more time, but he couldn't ignore what the guy said downstairs.

He had a feeling the warning was likely all hot air. But what if the guy found out where Nathan lived? He knew Mia was safe at Little Lambs, but he didn't like the idea of the guy wandering around his house.

He swallowed the last bite of his sandwich and cleared his throat. "Have you noticed a guy hanging around lately?" He went on to describe what the man looked like.

As he did so, Lynn's eyes widened, and she set her sandwich down, the food clearly forgotten. "Did Sharon tell you?"

"What? No, a man approached me downstairs. He warned me to stay away from you and all but threatened Mia and me." He studied Lynn's face closely. "Am I right to be concerned?" He expected her to say something. Instead, she pulled her phone out and started to text. "Lynn?"

"I'm letting Sharon know so she'll keep a close eye on Mia."

"Then I do need to worry." His chest tightened at the thought of some lunatic thinking he had the right to hurt someone else.

Lynn finished texting and slipped the phone back in her

pocket. She turned sad eyes to him. "I'm so sorry you've been dragged into this." With a resigned sigh, she leaned into the back of her chair. "I left the music industry for a lot of reasons. I missed my family, I was tired of the producers trying to make me bend my morals, and I was tired of having no space to myself. Especially when it came to one particular guy."

Nathan was all ears and motioned for her to continue.

"I think he might have followed the group around while we were touring. I always heard someone yell out that he loved me when I was going on stage for concerts. He'd leave flowers or candy for me at my bus. I ignored it, you know? Figured it was all part of the package. One of those things I had to deal with for living out my dream."

He clenched a fist. It didn't matter if Lynn was a pop star or the most normal person on the planet, no one deserved to be treated like that. "He was stalking you. What happened?"

"One night, he broke into my bus. Of course, he was stopped before he even got back to my room, but he managed to escape. That was just the last straw, you know? I'd kept rationalizing my decision to stay. But after that, I knew I had to do something else with my life. Get away from it all."

"Do you think this is the same guy?"

She nodded. "He's been leaving notes along with my old guitar picks on my car at work and on my front porch at home." She rubbed her arms as though she were warding off a sudden chill. "I think he's the reason why the press showed up at the restaurant and ambushed us."

Nathan tried to take it all in. If someone was stalking her, why didn't she tell him? "You should report all of this."

"I have. They've taken notes but said that, since he hasn't threatened me or trespassed, there's nothing they can do."

"We could put some cameras up to monitor your doors."

Lynn nodded. "We thought of that. Walt—Sharon's husband—put some up just this last week. Jeb has been careful enough to not come close ever since." She must have thought of something because her frown deepened. "I left for the hospital early, early this morning. How did he even know I was here unless he followed me? And if he followed me…"

"…then he was waiting outside your house, watching." Yeah, Nathan didn't like the sound of that. Judging by the way Lynn's face had paled, she didn't either. Was there seriously nothing the police could do? What would it take? Him breaking in and trying to hurt her first? "I think I'm going to stick around until you're ready to go home. Then a stop by the police department is in order. I'd like to let them know what Jeb said to me."

The thought that the guy might be lurking outside Lynn's house at night gave him the creeps and made him just plain mad. He'd love it if Jeb would follow Lynn right to the next jiu-jitsu class. Nathan would be happy to demonstrate a few choke-holds.

Lynn leaned forward and buried her face in her hands. "I'm so sorry I got you into this. I was hoping that, by lying low last week, he'd just leave me alone. I should've known better, though. I just wish he'd give up and go away." She lifted her chin, her watery eyes focusing on him. "If I'd told you about him before, then at least you'd have had a heads up."

There were a lot of things he wished had been handled differently, and the way she'd kept things to herself was one of them. He also had to admit a lot of this was the result of an extreme situation. One that he was certain even he wouldn't have known fully how to deal with.

He reached over and captured one of her hands in his. She squeezed back as though his hand were her lifeline. "Instead of beating yourself up over a situation you have no control over, why don't you just see this as a lesson in asking for help when you need it?" He stayed serious for several heartbeats before revealing a smile that he hoped would earn him one in return.

There. That pretty smile was exactly what he needed to see.

She ducked her chin again as pink colored her cheeks. "I admit it is a minor character flaw."

He nudged her in the arm. "Trust me, we all have them."

They still had a lot of things to talk about, and this Jeb guy was definitely a big concern, but Nathan felt more content sitting with Lynn now than he had the entire last week combined.

16

L ynn waited at the hospital long enough to see Perry again before she agreed to leave later that afternoon. She then drove behind Nathan to the police station where they filed a report. Nathan wasn't overly happy when he was also informed that they couldn't do anything about the man if he hadn't broken laws.

"This is ridiculous," Nathan said as they left the police station. "What does it take? The guy breaking into your house? Following you into Little Lambs? Breaking into my home? It shouldn't have to get to that."

Lynn couldn't agree more. It was all incredibly disheartening and overwhelming. Was it horrible that seeing Nathan so upset on her behalf was also reassuring and sweet?

It was, wasn't it? She probably shouldn't be thinking about any of that right now. Just because he'd stuck around for the day didn't mean their relationship was back to the way it was before.

What if he was only sticking around because he had a need to protect her?

Just like he would any other person he knew that needed help. He'd probably do this for Sharon, too.

In a moment, her bubble of comfort and hope burst. See, this was exactly what she was trying to avoid and why she'd hesitated to tell him any of this in the first place. He had Mia to worry about, and Lynn didn't want or need his pity.

Great, now she felt like crying. Oh, and she hadn't heard a word Nathan said in the last minute or so.

He leaned in a little to study her face. "Come on, let's go to your house where you can leave your car. Ride with me to Little Lambs. I can pick up Mia, you can talk to Sharon. Then I'll bring you back home."

Being home alone right now was the last thing Lynn wanted. It was probably selfish to agree to his plans, but she nodded all the same.

She couldn't help but scan the road or glance at the cars behind them. If the frequency with which Nathan checked his rearview mirror was any indication, he felt the same way.

At her house, Nathan made sure her cameras were still in working order, waited for her to give Thai a little attention, and then they headed back out again.

When they entered Little Lambs, Sharon finished talking to one of the families and hurried over. Her arms surrounded Lynn in a tight hug.

"What a day you've had. How's your sister? So Jeb followed you to the hospital?" As she asked her questions, she linked arms with Lynn and motioned for Nathan to follow. She led them into the back room where Mia's eyes lit up when she saw them.

She toddled, full speed, into her daddy's arms. But as soon as she'd received her hug, she was reaching for Lynn, too—a sweet gesture that had Lynn's eyes swimming with tears again. Man, she'd cried more today than the last year combined.

"It's good to see you, too, bug. I've missed you." Lynn pressed a kiss to the little girl's cheek and was more than happy to hold the girl close.

Sharon folded her arms and looked from Lynn to Nathan. "So what happened today with Jeb?"

Nathan filled her in, including some of the details he'd left out when he'd called earlier that day to check on Mia.

Lynn told her about going to the police department and filing another report.

Sharon shook her head. "That's it. You're coming to stay with me and Walt for a while."

"That's not a bad idea," Nathan agreed. "At least we don't have to worry about you at your place alone."

"Exactly," Sharon added with a definitive nod.

Lynn held Mia close and rubbed her back. "I'm not going anywhere." Her words snagged their attention and earned her a look of disapproval from both of them. "This guy has been bothering me for years. What am I supposed to do? Hide at your house, Sharon, for two or three more?"

Mia squirmed so Lynn set her back down again. The little girl made a beeline for the toys.

After watching her for several moments, Lynn turned again to her friends. "Look, Jeb creeps me out. I don't like feeling as though he's there watching me at all times. But I have to live my life. My windows are double paned and locked, both of my doors have deadbolts, and I've got cameras above them. The only thing I'm missing is a watchdog."

"But you do have a killer rolling pin," Sharon reminded her with an amused smile.

"That's right. I do have that." Lynn chuckled a little and

shrugged. "The situation isn't ideal, but it is what it is. If there's one thing Jeb's proved, it's that he doesn't quit. And I'm not willing to have him control my life because he doesn't have one of his own." She planted her hands on her hips for emphasis.

Sharon frowned but didn't argue. Nathan's expression was a mix of disapproval and respect. They looked at each other. "I guess that's that," Sharon said. "But promise me you'll call if you need anything."

"Of course." Lynn reached to give her friend a hug. "I do appreciate the offer to stay with you."

"And it's open any time, just say the word."

Mia didn't stay interested in the toys for long before she was back and fussing at her daddy's feet. Nathan scooped her up in his arms. "I'm pretty sure this little gal is hungry. We'd better get going." He nodded to Lynn. "I'll drop you back off at your place."

"Sounds good." Lynn turned and hugged her friend again. "I'll see you here tomorrow morning. I'll drive myself since I plan on leaving from here to go back to the hospital."

Sharon agreed. She smiled and waved goodbye as they made their way out.

Once she'd secured her seatbelt, Lynn covered a yawn as exhaustion set in. She'd dozed a little at the hospital earlier this morning, but otherwise, she'd been awake since before two. She planned on eating a sandwich, calling the hospital for an update on Perry, and then getting some sleep.

Nathan pulled up to Lynn's place. "I know this probably sounds silly, but if you'll give me your keys, I'll check your place out first. Make sure Jeb hasn't messed with it."

Lynn handed him her keys and then grinned as he walked up to her house. She turned to look at Mia in the back seat. "Your daddy sure is a gentleman. Did you know that?" She reached back and tweaked the little girl's knee, earning herself a giggle. "Yes, he is."

She scanned the street in front of her house, noting the cars. She wished she'd made more of a point to know her neighbors. It'd be easier to spot a car that wasn't supposed to be here. If she could get a license plate, it would help.

Nathan returned and opened the passenger door before handing the keys to Lynn. "Everything's all clear. If something comes up and you're worried, call me, okay?"

She nodded but Nathan ducked his head to look into her eyes. "I mean it." He ran a hand through his hair. "I've been meaning to ask...Can I still call you Lynn? Or would you prefer Bethany?"

"I'd love it if you called me Lynn."

He nodded, a hint of relief in his eyes. "I can understand why you left the music industry behind. I can even get why you changed your name and tried to start over again." He paused. "But I have to ask: If things only get harder now that Jeb knows where you are, is leaving again an option?"

"No." She didn't even have to think about it. "I've built my life here, and I have no intention of letting that go. I may have to deal with some things I tried to escape from, but I suppose that was going to happen eventually." Lynn gave him a reassuring smile. "I'm not going anywhere." She held her breath then, hoping and praying the same would be true for him. That he'd be willing to weather the difficult days ahead —preferably together.

He smiled in return. "Good. I'd better get Mia home."

She wished he didn't have to go. "Thanks for everything today. For the hospital, the ride, and for clearing my place." She waved goodbye to Mia before getting out and closing the door behind her. Nathan stood close enough for Lynn to get a whiff of his aftershave. Memories of what it was like to be held in his arms came flying back. She needed to get inside before she made a fool of herself. "I hope you and Mia have a good night."

"You, too, Lynn. Be careful." He studied her for several moments as though he were going to say something else.

Only when he dropped his arms to his sides did Lynn give another nod. "I'll see you and Mia at Little Lambs tomorrow." With one more attempt at a normal smile, she turned and started up the driveway. She was glad they'd had a chance to talk a little, but she wished she knew where his head was. Was he still struggling with what the future might hold?

She hadn't gone more than a few steps when she heard her name followed by Nathan's arm on her shoulder. His hand slid down to hers where he clasped it gently and tugged her around to face him.

Without a word, he leaned in with the softest, sweetest kiss she'd ever experienced. It lasted only a handful of seconds, but it was enough to turn her legs into jelly.

"I'll see you tomorrow."

Certain at least twenty pounds had been lifted off her shoulders, Lynn reluctantly walked away from Nathan and went inside. After closing and locking her door, she leaned against it and released a happy sigh. Maybe they really did have a chance of surviving this together.

Thai rubbed against her legs with a meow. Lynn leaned over to pick him up. "Sorry, buddy. I guess I'm a little distracted," she said with a dreamy smile.

JEB SLAMMED his binoculars against the center console of his car and cursed. After everything today, the guy still had the audacity to go after her? Jeb had half a mind to walk down the street right now and prove to Bethany exactly why she should be with him instead.

But the more he thought about it, the more he realized he needed to get Bethany alone. Talk some sense into her. Surely then she'd see why he was the better choice.

He just had to figure out the details.

IT WAS anything but easy for Nathan to drive away and leave Lynn at her house. Even though he scanned the street as he left, he couldn't help but feel like he was leaving Lynn at the mercy of the psychopath who wouldn't leave her alone. He'd be feeling much more relaxed if she'd agreed to stay with Sharon.

He had to admire her, though, for standing up to her stalker and not letting him completely change her life. A lot of people wouldn't have the guts.

Her tenacity was only one of many things he admired about her.

Maybe it was foolish to have kissed her before they had a chance to iron everything out. There were a lot of things he wanted to know—questions he wanted to ask. But she'd been adorable, with that look of vulnerability and uncertainty in her eyes. He couldn't let her walk away like that. Especially when he understood how she felt. The situation wasn't easy —not by a long shot. Choosing to kiss her, though? He wished he was as certain about every other decision he had to make.

If Mia hadn't been waiting on him, he no doubt would've gathered Lynn into his arms right there in the driveway and kissed her until they were both breathless.

Just thinking about it had him smiling.

He'd figure out a way to see her soon. If there was one thing that their week apart taught him, it was that he didn't want another one like it.

Mia whined from the back seat, bringing Nathan to the present. "Sorry, baby. We're going. Let's get you home."

As he pulled away from Lynn's house, he prayed for protection not only for Lynn but for himself and Mia as well. The stalker had been focused on Lynn for years, he was bound to make a mistake soon.

Nathan could only hope to be there when he did.

17

L ynn entered work with a smile on her face the next day, a detail Sharon immediately noted.

"Someone's in a good mood."

Lynn shrugged as she put her stuff up and got ready for the day. She lowered her voice. "No sign of my stalker, and Nathan kissed me after he took me home last night. So yeah, I guess I am in a good mood."

Sharon grinned then. "Oh, I'm so glad. Does that mean you two are okay then?"

Unfortunately, Lynn wasn't sure what it meant. But at least it was a sign they were moving in the right direction. She told Sharon as much. "I wish I knew for sure. I have to make sure I get in to see my sister this evening. Otherwise I'd see if Nathan and I could meet and talk."

"Things are weird right now. You two will figure it out." Sharon winked.

For the first time in days, Lynn really felt her friend might be right.

She only saw Nathan for a few minutes when he brought Mia by before he was off to work. The day went well and was

160 MELANIE D. SNITKER

uneventful—just the way Lynn preferred. Before she knew it, it was evening and Nathan was back to pick up his daughter.

"Are you going to head over and see your sister next?"

Lynn nodded. "I figured I'd swing through somewhere and grab a sandwich to eat on the way. I'd take her something to eat, except she may be on a restricted diet. Then do I pick something up for my parents or not? Way too complicated. So I'll see how she's doing and maybe run down to the gift shop and get her a balloon or some flowers or something like that."

"That sounds like a good plan." Nathan picked up Mia and settled her in his arms. "I'm going to take this munchkin home. If you need anything, call me."

The way he looked at her then, Lynn had a feeling he would've kissed her if they'd been somewhere besides Little Lambs. She wished they were somewhere else.

"I will. You two have a relaxing evening. Would it be okay if I call later and let you know how the visit went?"

Nathan's face brightened. "Of course. I'll be looking forward to it."

Lynn waved as they left and then released a happy sigh.

Sharon came up and nudged her shoulder. "Keep that happy feeling when you see your parents in a while."

Lynn scowled at her. "You just had to mention them. Are you trying to depress me?" She chuckled. "Truthfully, I'm going to see my sister and talk to Nathan tonight. I won't let my parents get to me."

And she maintained that attitude all the way to the hospital. Her parents were nowhere to be seen in the waiting area, so she went to Perry's room only to find it was empty.

Fear and panic gripped her as she dashed down the hall to the nurse's station. "Where is Perry Truitt? I just went by her room and she wasn't there."

"Oh! I'm sorry—are you a member of the family?"

"Yes, I'm her sister. I was coming by this evening to check on her."

The nurse pulled something up on the computer. "Ah, yes. She was moved to a different room. You'll find her in 823. Go down the hall, take the first right, and then the room will be on the left."

"Thank you." Lynn hoped this meant Perry was doing better than the doctor expected. When she found the room, her parents were inside. They glanced at her, and immediately her father shifted his attention to his phone.

With some effort, Lynn ignored it, offered her mother a small smile, and then walked up to the other side of Perry's bed. To her relief, Perry was sitting up. She waved, and Lynn gave her a gentle hug. "How are you feeling? Any better?"

Perry nodded. "A little bit, but I keep getting tired." As if for emphasis, she yawned. It wasn't for show, though. There were dark circles under her eyes and a sleepiness about them.

Lynn leaned over again and gave her another hug. "I know. It's a good thing, though. While you're sleeping, your body is working overtime to help you feel better again soon."

It was still really hard to see her normally-energetic sister so quiet and still.

The door opened and a nurse came in with a smile on her face. "How are we doing in here? Are you ready for me to change your bandages? Then we'll have some food brought up for you."

Originally, the mention of changing bandages had a frown on Perry's face, but the idea of eating dinner seemed to erase some of that.

The nurse gave them all an apologetic smile. "If I could have everyone step outside for a minute, that would be great."

Lynn led the way into the hall and then their group of

three shuffled a little to get out of the way while they waited. She lowered her voice. "So is she really doing okay?"

Mom nodded, although there was a shadow of concern on her face. "She is. I hate seeing her so tired after doing any little thing. Just the act of eating wears her out."

Dad spoke from his position, nearly startling Lynn. "The doctor said it's normal, and that it can take as long as six months before she's feeling herself again."

Dad said actual words to her. To relay something helpful. Lynn could hardly believe her ears.

He looked at her then. "You shouldn't come tomorrow after you get off work."

Lynn's eyes widened. "Look, I get you don't want me here. But I'm coming by every day she's in the hospital no matter what you say."

Dad held up a hand to stop her. "I'm not trying to get you to stay away. I'm just saying to wait and come by around seven. Last night she struggled to visit while eating and then fell asleep. By seven, she'll probably be awake again and on her second wind."

Lynn's gaze swiveled to Mom because she wasn't entirely sure she should believe her dad's suggestion. It was almost nice of him.

Mom smiled and nodded. She hid it well, but even Lynn could see that Mom was surprised by her husband's words as well.

"Okay." It actually made a lot of sense. "Sure. That'll give me time to go home, eat some dinner, and change clothes. Then maybe I can guarantee I don't have baby spit on my shirt." She'd washed the spots off, but that was never quite enough.

Mom chuckled. "Do you like your job at the day care center?"

"Are you kidding? I get paid to cuddle and play with a bunch of babies. What's not to love?" She meant that, too. There were always little things she'd like to change, but they were just that: little. "I take care of Nathan's daughter there. That's how we met." Just thinking about them made her heart flip flop in her chest.

"Are you two serious?" There was genuine interest in Mom's voice, and even though Dad wasn't commenting, it was clear he was listening.

"I hope so." She couldn't imagine not having them in her life. Her voice sounded wistful, even to her own ears.

The nurse came out then and motioned for them to go back inside. She gave them a quick report, assured Perry they'd be having food delivered soon, and left.

Lynn remembered what her dad said and told Perry, "I'm going to leave when your food gets here so you can eat." When Perry looked disappointed, Lynn added, "I'll be back tomorrow, but probably around seven, and I'll stay longer. Deal?"

"Deal."

While they waited for her food to be delivered, she mostly listened to Perry tell them all about a weird dream she'd had while she was asleep earlier, and how she couldn't wait to eat a cheeseburger again.

This time, when Lynn told her sister goodbye, she didn't feel nearly as sad about leaving. Thankfully, it was still light outside so finding her car was easy.

She was hungry again by the time she got home. After pouring herself a bowl of cereal, she got comfortable on her couch and quickly dialed Nathan's number.

Her pulse quickened the moment his voice came over the line. "Hey, you. How was your visit?"

"It went really well. My dad even spoke to me." She told

him about the evening. By the time she was done, her cereal was getting soggy. "How about you? How's everything going there?"

While Nathan told her about trying to get Mia bathed and his dishwasher going out, she ate her cereal and marveled about how she couldn't imagine a better way to end the night than talking with Nathan.

Well, maybe that and a good night kiss.

"I'M glad she's doing better, and that your dad was more open to you being there." Although Nathan was saddened that Lynn's dad *not* telling her to leave was such a huge improvement. He could only hope that God was slowly mending that family's relationship. "So you're going back tomorrow around seven?"

"Yes. They said that visiting hours are until nine, so I'll probably stay until then."

Nathan didn't like the idea of her leaving the hospital that late by herself, especially right after it gets dark. "Any sign of Jeb?"

She paused. "Not a thing. I've kept my eyes open, too. I'd like to hope he's gone, but years of history say that's not likely." The tone of her voice changed from being hopeful and happy to hesitant and worried.

Nathan hated that his question had taken some of her joy away. At the same time, it was a real worry, and he wanted to make sure Lynn kept alert. Especially if she was going to be out late. "I know. I'm sorry you have to keep dealing with this." He wished he could reach through the phone and hold her close.

"I was hoping we could have dinner soon. I'd say

tomorrow between work and going to the hospital would be good, but I promised Chess I'd come over and help him load some lumber right after I picked up Mia." Nathan thought a moment. "What about after work on Thursday? We could come to my house where it'll be easier to talk without worrying about interruptions."

There was almost no hesitation before she said, "That would be great." They settled on the time, visited a few more minutes, and then Nathan had to end the conversation to get Mia into bed. "I'll talk to you tomorrow," he told Lynn.

"You bet. Good night, Nathan."

"Good night."

He set his phone down and scooped Mia into his arms. "Are you ready for some sleeps, little girl?"

Mia shook her head at the same time as a giant yawn consumed her.

Nathan chuckled. "Come on, let's get some pajamas on. I'll bet you were glad to have Miss Lynn back today, weren't you?" He'd noticed Mia was clinging to Lynn when he picked her up from Little Lambs. He completely understood and sometimes envied Mia the opportunity to spend an entire day with Lynn. "So am I."

18

———————

Nathan wiped the sweat from his forehead after stacking the last bit of lumber. "You're going to have a busy weekend."

"Yep." Chess told him all about his plans to build a deck and trellis for Brooke over the weekend. "When we bought this place, the lack of a nice back porch was a big drawback. I figure the sooner we have one, the sooner we can start enjoying it."

"Makes sense." He didn't envy his brother the project, though Chess didn't seem to mind. He was the type of person that enjoyed putting all of his focus into one thing. "It was a good idea to have everything on hand so you can get up first thing on Saturday and start working on it."

Chess nodded. "I figure getting it done now before the summer heat truly hits will be good." He closed the gate to the backyard. "So what about you? What are your plans?"

"Tonight or this weekend?"

"Yes."

"Lynn and I are having dinner at my house tomorrow night so we can actually talk without fear of the stalker or the press showing up." Nathan had often wondered where they'd be now if they'd had a chance to really talk that night at the restaurant. "This evening, she's going to see her sister at the hospital. I wish she weren't going quite so late though. It's horrible, but I just picture the stalker waiting for her around every corner."

Chess looked concerned. "It's a valid worry. How late is she planning on staying?"

"Until visiting hours end at nine."

Chess's expression mirrored Nathan's thoughts on the situation.

Brooke spoke up from her spot on the tiny porch where she stood holding Mia. "Unless she got a spot close to the hospital, that parking lot is terrible, too." Mia pointed at the pile of wood with interest.

That didn't make Nathan feel any better. Maybe he could take Mia over there and meet up with Lynn and walk her to her car. At least then he'd know she got there okay.

His thoughts must have been evident on his face because Brooke rubbed the little girl's back and said, "Just leave Mia with us. You can swing by and pick her up on the way home."

Nathan might have objected except they'd kept Mia many times in the past. His daughter always slept well and enjoyed spending time with her aunt and uncle. "If you guys are sure, I might do that. I keep worrying about Lynn today, and I'm not sure why."

"Then follow your instinct and go check on your girl." Chess winked. "Did you still want to stay for dinner, or head over now?"

Nathan checked his watch. It was just after seven. Lynn would be with Perry now. He didn't want to interrupt the visit. "I can stay for dinner. I'll just head that way afterward. Besides, I've been smelling Brooke's chicken parmesan all evening. My stomach will never forgive me if I walk away from it now."

Brooke smiled brightly. "I'm glad you can stay. Dinner should be ready in about fifteen minutes if you guys want to get cleaned up."

Chess dusted his hands off on his pants. "You don't have to tell me twice."

Nathan agreed. He'd been looking forward to the meal, and now that he knew he'd be meeting up with Lynn later, he could relax more and enjoy it.

An hour later, Nathan pulled into the large hospital parking lot only to find it was full. It left him no choice but to drive into the large parking garage and begin the search for an open space. He finally found one but never did see Lynn's car.

Once inside, Nathan thought about texting Lynn to let her know he was there, but then figured she might have her phone off if she was in with Perry anyway. Instead, he opted to surprise her.

Thankfully, Lynn had texted him earlier and let him know about Perry's room change. It didn't take him long to locate it. Afraid to interrupt or wake Perry if she were sleeping, he tapped lightly on the door. Moments later, it opened.

Nathan found himself face to face with Mr. Truitt. "Good evening, sir. I was looking for Lynn. Could I speak to her for a moment, please?"

Mr. Truitt opened the door wide enough for Nathan to see that Lynn wasn't inside. "You just missed her."

Mrs. Truitt leaned over so she could see him better. "She said she felt like she might be coming down with a cold and didn't want to get Perry sick, so she left early. I'm surprised you two didn't pass each other."

Catching up with Lynn shouldn't be a big deal, but a ball

of dread formed in his gut and he pushed back a sense of urgency. "Do you happen to know where she parked?"

Mr. Truitt nodded once. "She'd mentioned she had to park on the sixth floor of the parking garage." His eyes narrowed. "Is everything okay?"

"Of course. I'm so sorry to have bothered you all. I'm going to see if I can catch up with her." He waved at Perry. "I'm happy to hear you're feeling better. I'm praying for you daily."

The young woman's eyes lit up as she smiled and waved in return. "Thank you."

With a last courteous nod to both of Lynn's parents, he turned and jogged to the elevator.

He couldn't explain it, but something was wrong. "Please, Father, place a hedge of protection around Lynn right now and guide my steps as I try to find her."

LYNN CLEARED HER THROAT, more than a little annoyed at herself and the timing of this summer cold. Or whatever was going on. She didn't feel bad necessarily, but her throat was scratchy and she had that heavy feeling in her eyes that always signaled an illness of some kind was incoming.

It'd been incredibly disappointing to have to leave early and not stay with Perry for a while tonight. But she'd still gone in to say hi and explain why she couldn't stay long. And she'd rather leave than risk getting Perry sick, making it more difficult for her to recover.

If Lynn felt better tomorrow, she'd go back again. For now, what she really needed was to get home and sleep. Maybe some extra rest would help her avoid whatever this was.

First, she had to traverse the walk back to her car. The parking was one thing she disliked about this hospital. Unless you wanted to pay for valet parking, the parking garage was almost always the only choice.

She went down to the fifth floor of the hospital and walked to the opposite side where a sky bridge connected it with the parking garage's fifth floor.

The moment she pushed the door open and stepped into the parking garage, the air hit her face. It was warmer than the hospital, but not quite as hot as it'd been earlier in the day. She could easily see where she was going, but the sunlight was waning, giving the quiet parking garage an eerie feel.

Lynn swallowed hard, her scratchy throat reminding her of her goal to get home again. Instead of walking up the stairs to the sixth floor, she decided to take the elevator. At least she hadn't parked too far away from where the elevator was located on the next floor.

Once inside, she breathed a sigh of relief, hit the correct button, and leaned against the wall. The doors began to slide shut, but stopped moments before closing.

Lynn's attention jumped to the doors and the hand that was in between them. When they opened again, a man stepped inside. She didn't think anything of it at first, except to wonder why he was in such a hurry and didn't just wait for the elevator to come back.

He had a baseball cap on that was pulled down far enough to partially block his face.

It wasn't until the elevator doors closed completely and started moving that he pushed the bill of his hat up and looked at her with piercing eyes.

The same eyes as the man who'd delivered her pizza that had been tampered with.

Jeb.

Oh, God. Help me keep calm.

There was no way she hadn't revealed that she knew who he was. The corners of his mouth lifted a little as though he were happy she recognized him. She gripped her handbag with both hands and shifted it in front of her.

How were they not at the sixth floor yet?

Just as the elevator began to slow, Jeb reached out and hit the stop button, effectively halting Lynn's mode of escape.

Her pulse thundered in her ears as her stomach fell to the floor. Her gaze darted to the emergency call button on the elevator wall.

Jeb must have noticed because he shifted his body to stand between her and the only real means of calling for help. "Not so fast, Bethany. It's time you and I had a little heart-to-heart."

It was the last thing she wanted. She wished she'd taken the stairs. He'd probably been following her, but at least she could try and run. Right now, she was just as caged as a hunted rabbit caught in a trap.

She tried to calm her racing mind. *Think, Lynn, think.* The guy had been stalking her for years. He was clearly infatuated with her, and more than a little insane. She had to do something to keep him from going to the offensive.

"Are you the one that kept leaving me the notes?" His eyes lit up as though he were excited she'd finally made a connection. "I can't believe you kept those guitar picks all those years." *Smile, Lynn. Just try to play along.*

"I have a whole bag of them." He sobered, and he stared at her as though he were trying to make up his mind about something. "Nothing was the same after you left, Bethany. All I had were the guitar picks and the videos. You should have let me know where you went. How could you not?"

It was clear he'd created a whole story in his head, which

was more dangerous because that meant Lynn had no real idea exactly what role she'd played in it. Clearly, he'd imagined them having a relationship of some kind before she left the music industry, which meant he felt like she'd dumped him without any explanation.

"I'm sorry I didn't tell you where I went. There were so many people bothering me all the time. It made it impossible to focus on the ones who really mattered." It was all she could do to keep the disgust off her face as she spoke. "I had to get some space. Clear my head."

"You could've contacted me. I wouldn't have told a soul."

Lynn was certain he was the one responsible for leaking her whereabouts. She had no doubt that, if he'd known where she was back then, he would've shouted it to everyone just to prove his status. "I'm sorry, Jeb. I didn't mean to hurt you."

That much was true. She'd left to escape him and everything else related to the music industry. She hadn't done so specifically to hurt anyone. She'd had no idea he'd spent the last few years looking for her. Who could have?

Her words seemed to placate him and he relaxed a little.

Lynn looked at the elevator door and back tor Jeb. "It's getting pretty hot in here, and someone else is going to need the elevator and call to say it's broken. What do you say we get out of here?" Maybe, when the doors opened, there'd be someone else waiting. If Lynn screamed for help and made a scene, Jeb might run. She got the impression he was much more of a coward than a confrontational person. That could definitely work in her favor.

Jeb's eyes narrowed as he studied her face. "My car is a few spots down from the elevator. When we get out, you're coming with me. We have a lot of time to make up for, Bethany, and I don't want to waste another day."

He said the words as though he were discussing the

weather instead of her potential abduction. His tone and the lack of emotion in his eyes sent chills down Lynn's spine.

Jeb reached out and grasped her arm with one hand, squeezing hard enough to make Lynn flinch. When she tried to move her arm away, he only squeezed tighter. He pushed a button and finally the elevator reached its destination.

Get me out of this, God. Please.

As soon as the doors opened, Lynn looked around, desperately praying someone else would be there to help her. Her heart sank when she realized there wasn't a soul.

Jeb turned right as they exited the elevator and began to pull her along beside him.

If he got her in his car, she may never get away alive.

The realization had her screaming with every ounce of strength in her body, "Someone! Please, help me! Help!"

Jeb whirled and slapped her hard enough that Lynn stumbled. She licked the corner of her mouth and tasted her own blood. He pointed a finger at her. "You shut up, or I'll knock you again." This time, when he jerked her arm, she whimpered with pain. "You're just like the rest of them, you know that? But once you get to know me, you'll change. You'll see you love me."

Lynn had no way of knowing how much further they had to go before they'd reach his car. All she knew was that if she didn't get away now, she was going to become one of those women who is kidnapped and found years and years later, only a shell of the person she was before.

That was *not* going to happen to her.

One of the moves she'd learned in Nathan's class came to mind. She might not be proficient enough to hold Jeb, but she could at least knock him off balance. Anything she could do to buy time.

At that moment, her phone pinged, momentarily

distracting Jeb. Without warning, she allowed herself to drop to the ground. Then she threaded her legs through his, causing Jeb to slam into the pavement with a grunt. He lost his grip on her arm, and Lynn pulled it free. "Someone! Help me! Please!"

Jeb swore as he tried to roll away from her. When her attempts to pin him down angered him further, he tried to backhand her. His position was just awkward enough that Lynn was able to avoid contact.

He wrestled with her, and with each movement, she could feel her control slip. Time was running out. Jeb seethed with anger as he pulled free and turned on her.

Dear God, save me.

———

NATHAN PUNCHED the elevator button multiple times. The sense of urgency he'd felt in the hospital only intensified here in the parking garage, and he decided to take the stairs. He took his cell phone out and sent Lynn a quick text. "You okay? I'm in the parking garage on my way to the sixth floor. Let me know." Then he set about taking the stairs two at a time.

He was halfway up when Lynn's voice carried to him, her tone high with terror.

"Someone! Help me! Please!"

Nathan wasn't sure how he got to the top of the stairs, but as soon as he did, he saw two people wrestling on the ground maybe fifteen cars away. He ran, the sounds of his shoes echoing off the concrete all around them.

He got close enough to see that Jeb had Lynn by her hair and was using it to make her stand again, both of them with their backs to Nathan. "Hey, Jeb!" The moment the creep turned around, Nathan landed a punch on the man's jaw, his own hand aching at the contact. It accomplished exactly what Nathan needed it to: Jeb let go of Lynn's hair.

Nathan looked to her just long enough to see the blood on the corner of her mouth and the bruise forming on her cheek. That was all it took for renewed energy to flow through his body.

Jeb swung at him with a punch that was easy for Nathan to dodge. Even with the guy standing several inches taller than Nathan, and weighing a good thirty pounds more, Nathan could tell this wouldn't even be a challenge.

He just had to get control of Jeb long enough for the police to get here.

As if she were reading his mind, Lynn pulled her phone out, dialed something, and within seconds he heard her say, "Yes, a man tried to abduct me and is attempting to hurt someone else."

That was all Nathan heard. It was enough that she was getting help. His job was to make sure Jeb was still here when that help arrived.

Jeb tried to punch Nathan again. It was easily deflected, but it was just enough to take Nathan's anger to the next level.

"Enough!" With a calculated dive, Nathan went for both of Jeb's legs, using the man's own weight and momentum to flip him through the air and onto his back. Jeb struggled, grabbing Nathan's shirt, his fists flailing.

Now that Nathan had Jeb on the ground, years of jiu-jitsu training kicked in as naturally as breathing. It took no time for Nathan to pin him down by placing his right leg across Jeb's face, the other leg across his chest, and then pull and twist Jeb's arm back in an armbar that had the man howling in pain. Every time Jeb tried to move or fight back, Nathan pulled just a little harder, and his captive could only whimper.

Nathan might have smiled at the man's discomfort if he weren't so angry. "You have no idea how easily I could send you to the hospital instead of jail."

The words were just loud enough for Jeb to hear, and the man's eyes widened.

Nathan turned his head. "Lynn. Are you okay?"

"I'll be fine. They are sending police now, and are contacting security here at the hospital. Someone should be here soon."

"Good." Nathan pulled on Jeb's arm again, and the sound of the man screaming did make Nathan feel a little bit better. "Although I could do this all night." When Jeb twisted his neck to look at him, Nathan gave him a smile.

Jeb howled in rage before turning his attention to Lynn. "I love you, Bethany. Why can't you see that? I love you."

The sound of multiple sets of shoes on the pavement pulled Nathan's attention to the three security guards approaching. One of them pulled a gun and leveled it at Jeb. Another officer withdrew a set of handcuffs and quickly took over control of Jeb, giving Nathan the room to stand again.

The moment he did, he strode to where Lynn leaned against a support beam. The fear in her eyes faded to relief as she pushed away from it, her hands trembling. "Nathan…"

He reached for her then and wrapped his arms around her. "Shhhh…it's over."

"Oh, this isn't over!" Jeb yelled from his position on the ground. Even with his hands in cuffs and three officers surrounding him, his smile spoke of confidence. "This is all a big mistake. I did nothing, and I'll be back out again in forty-eight hours. Mark my words."

Nathan nodded toward the video camera near the ceiling

maybe fifteen feet from their location. "Something tells me we'll have plenty of evidence to prove otherwise."

It was satisfying to see Jeb look at the camera and struggle only to have an officer push him to his knees on the pavement. The sound of sirens somewhere in the parking structure signaled the arrival of backup that would ensure Jeb would be going straight to a police station downtown.

Nathan turned his entire focus toward Lynn, his heart aching and anger burning as he took in the small cut at the corner of her mouth, the tinge of purple on her cheek, and the obvious finger-shaped bruises on her arm. He took a handkerchief out of his back pocket and gently dabbed at her cut to wipe away the blood. "I'm so sorry I didn't get here sooner. We should take you inside and have you checked out."

Lynn looked into his eyes. "You saved my life." She swallowed hard then took in a shaky breath as the reality of what just happened seemed to hit her hard. "If you hadn't..."

"Hey, don't do that." Nathan pulled her close, relishing the feel of her warmth. "Don't give him any more control by imagining what might have happened. You're safe now. We're going to make sure he never bothers you again." He gently cupped her face in both of his hands. "I love you, Lynn. I should've told you long before now." She gasped, but he plowed again. "When I found out who you really were, I worried you'd get up and leave. Change your name and disappear like you did before."

Lynn slowly shook her head as a tear slipped from the corner of her eye. "And I thought once you knew who I was, that you'd walk away just like everyone else has. I couldn't bear that because you and Mia mean so much to me. I love you, too, Nathan."

Nathan cupped her face in his hands and affectionately touched the dimple in her chin with one thumb. "Why don't we agree that, no matter what our future holds, we always go through it together?"

"I like the sound of that."

He leaned in, desperately needing to kiss her.

He'd only had a moment to taste her lips when Lynn's eyes flew open as she pulled away. "I wasn't feeling well earlier. I might be getting a cold…"

Nathan chuckled. "Honey, I couldn't care less."

With that, he closed the gap again and relished the way she fit so perfectly in his arms. Everything about her, from the scent of her hair to how her lips danced with his, only proved she was made for him. He had no intention of ever letting her go.

EPILOGUE

NINE MONTHS LATER

Lynn poured sparkling grape juice into the sixth wine glass. She, Brooke, and Anna each grabbed two and hurried through the back door and onto the large wooden deck. Stars shone overhead in the clear sky.

She smiled as Nathan snagged one of the glasses, then wrapped a warm arm around her waist. With his other hand, he lifted hers and pressed a kiss to the wedding band on her finger. The chilly weather seemed eager to welcome a new year. It was a good thing Mia had fallen asleep hours ago and was resting inside where it was nice and warm. "How much longer?"

Chess answered from his spot on the deck where he was holding Brooke close. "Three more minutes until midnight."

Joel accepted a glass from Anna and gave her a kiss before addressing their little group. "Can I just say this may be the best new year yet. God has blessed us all in more ways than we could count. We celebrated two weddings last year," he nodded first toward Chess and Brooke and then at Nathan and Lynn, "there's a precious, healthy little girl asleep inside, and we have new life joining our family this spring." He placed his palm against Anna's growing belly.

Chess nodded. "If there's one thing we've all learned, it's that we can't control the curveballs life throws at us. And goodness knows there have been a bunch of them."

Nathan couldn't agree more. "But we can choose what team we play for." He held his glass in the air.

The arrival of midnight was announced by the sounds of fireworks and whoops from the neighbors.

Lynn and the others joined Nathan in raising their glasses.

"To being surrounded by family!" Chess said.

"Uncountable blessings," Joel added.

Nathan put an arm around Lynn and drew her close. "And the chance to start anew."

"Amen," Lynn whispered as tears gathered in her eyes.

"Happy New Year!" They all yelled in unison.

Nathan clinked glasses with Lynn, and they both took a sip. He set their glasses on a nearby table before pulling her close and placing a small kiss on her chin. "I am so in love with you, Lynn Kirkpatrick."

Lynn clasped her hands together behind his back as she leaned into his warmth. "I love you, too."

He kissed her thoroughly then, and Lynn no longer noticed the cold air. The only fireworks that registered were the ones between her and the man she looked forward to spending the rest of her life with—a life that held more promise than she ever dreamed possible.

A Note from the Author

WHEN I FIRST BEGAN THE Love Unexpected series, I had no idea it would contain some of the most challenging—and most rewarding—books I've ever written. Now that the third, and final book, is finished, I find myself having trouble saying goodbye to these characters. It is my hope that they've grown to become as real to you as they have to me.

I think all of us can relate to at least some of the struggles that Joel and Anna, Chess and Brooke, and Nathan and Lynn experienced in their lives. It's true that biological family is important. For better or worse, we wouldn't be who we are without them. But sometimes the other people that God places in our lives leave just as much of an impact.

Isn't it comforting to know that we have a Father in heaven who sees us and loves us, even when it feels like no one else does? May we all be thankful for the people He chooses to bless us with, and may we hope and pray that He will use us to be that source of encouragement and hope in the lives of others.

IF YOU ENJOYED the Love Unexpected series, I think you'd like the new series Danger in Destiny. Grab the first book, **Out of the Ashes**, today!

He thought it was just a structure fire.

As a firefighter, Bryce Keyes is no stranger when it comes to running into a burning building. What he didn't expect was coming face-to-face with the woman he loved years ago. Getting her out safely is one thing, but when it looks like she was the arsonist's target, Bryce realizes he can't just let her walk away again. Especially not while her life is in danger.

She's desperate to escape.

For Megan Bristow, returning to Destiny, Texas was about saying a final goodbye to a dysfunctional family and the memories she's tried hard to bury. She planned to go in, help her mother tie up loose ends, and get out again. When someone makes an attempt on her life, Megan realizes those loose ends are only the beginning of a tangled web, and she's been drawn right into the center of it.

They'll have to put the past behind them.

Only by working together will they be able to figure out who's hunting her and why - before it's too late.

Read Out of the Ashes

Want a FREE BOOK?
Sign up for Melanie D. Snitker's
newsletter and get a **FREE** novella!
Sign up today!

SPECIAL THANKS

First and foremost, I want to praise You, God, not only for the opportunity to write *Starting Anew*, but for the many blessings the process has brought me. It took much longer to write Nathan and Lynn's story than I'd ever planned on. Looking back, however, I wouldn't change a thing. Thank you for being faithful. Even though the seasons in my life are always shifting, You never fail to be the constant that keeps me grounded. Thank you for using this book, and the last two years, to remind me of that.

Doug, you know that this series has been anything but easy for me to write, and I couldn't have finished it if it weren't for your patience and encouragement. I'm so thankful God orchestrated a number of things that made it possible for us to meet, fall in love, and be a part of an amazing family together.

To my readers, thank you for taking time out of your day to make Nathan and Lynn a part of your book family. I appreciate each and every one of you.

Steph, you and your family are such a blessing. God brought our families together. Your insight on my books is priceless, but your friendship even more so.

Krista, thank you so much for fitting my book baby into your editing schedule. You've been patient, encouraging, and your editing skills just rock. I appreciate you!

ABOUT THE AUTHOR

Melanie D. Snitker is a *USA Today* bestselling author who writes inspirational romance and romantic suspense. She and her husband live in Texas with their two children. They share their home with three dogs and a variety of small animals. In her spare time, Melanie enjoys photography, reading, training her dog, playing computer games, and hanging out with family and friends.

https://www.melaniedsnitker.com/

BOOKS BY MELANIE D. SNITKER

Danger in Destiny

Out of the Ashes

Frozen in Jeopardy

Healing Hearts

Calming the Storm

I Still Do

Don't Kiss Me Goodbye

Love Unexpected

Safe In His Arms

Someone to Trust

Starting Anew

Love's Compass

Finding Peace

Finding Hope

Finding Courage

Finding Faith

Finding Joy

Finding Grace

BOOKS BY MELANIE D. SNITKER

For a complete list of books

www.melaniedsnitker.com